T0006036

WANDERING
SOULS

WANDERING SOULS

A NOVEL

CECILE PIN

HENRY HOLT AND COMPANY

NEW YORK

Henry Holt and Company
Publishers since 1866
120 Broadway
New York, New York 10271
www.henryholt.com

Henry Holt® and ⓗ ® are registered trademarks of Macmillan
Publishing Group, LLC.

Library of Congress Cataloging-in-Publication Data

Names: Pin, Cecile, author.
Title: Wandering souls : a novel / Cecile Pin.
Description: First US edition. | New York : Henry Holt and
    Company, 2023.
Identifiers: LCCN 2022052638 (print) | LCCN 2022052639
    (ebook) | ISBN 9781250863461 (hardcover) | ISBN 9781250863478
    (ebook)
Subjects: LCGFT: Fiction. | Novels.
Classification: LCC PR6116.I664 W36 2023 (print) |
    LCC PR6116.I664 (ebook) | DDC 823/.92—dc23/eng/20221128
LC record available at https://lccn.loc.gov/2022052638
LC ebook record available at https://lccn.loc.gov/2022052639

Our books may be purchased in bulk for promotional, educational, or
business use. Please contact your local bookseller or the Macmillan
Corporate and Premium Sales Department at (800) 221–7945, extension
5442, or by e-mail at MacmillanSpecialMarkets@macmillan.com.

First US Edition 2023

Designed by Omar Chapa

Printed in the United States of America

1   3   5   7   9   10   8   6   4   2

And she gave birth to a son, and Moses named him Gershom, for he said, "I have been a stranger in a strange land."

EXODUS 2:22

Watching their little bodies, I wondered where grief gets lodged in such small vessels.

MAGGIE NELSON,

THE RED PARTS

WANDERING
SOULS

PART I

1

November 1978—Vung Tham, Vietnam

There are the goodbyes and then the fishing out of the bodies—everything in between is speculation.

In the years to come, Thi Anh would let the harrowing memories of the boat and the camp trickle out of her until they were nothing but a whisper. But she would hold on to that last evening with all her might, from the smell of the steaming rice in the kitchen to the touch of her mother's skin as she embraced her for the last time.

Her mother, she would remember, preparing her daughter's favorite dish, caramelized braised pork and eggs, humming "Tous les garçons et les filles" by Françoise Hardy. The French had left Vietnam twenty-five years prior, but their music still lingered, the yé-yé melodies filling the homes of the village of Vung Tham. Anh was filling her backpack in the bedroom next door, debating what to bring and what to leave behind. "Pack lightly," her father had told her. "There won't be much room on the boat." She held her school uniform to her chest, a pleated skirt and a white shirt whose sleeves were too short for her sixteen-year-old arms, and placed it in her bag.

Her brothers Thanh and Minh were doing the same in the bedroom across from hers, their belongings scattered across the tiled floor, and she could hear them arguing. They had to share a backpack between them, and Thanh maintained that because his clothes were slightly smaller, as he was ten and Minh was thirteen, Minh should pack fewer items than him. "Your clothes take too much space. It's only fair if I pack more than you." Their mother went to the room to investigate the noise, the smell of the caramelized pork following her. As Thanh began to explain the problem to her, his voice faded, her exasperated face quieting his trivial concern. "Sorry," he muttered as Minh looked at him with a triumphant smile. "It doesn't matter."

Through her opened door, Anh saw their younger brother Dao watching the quarrel unfold from the edge of his futon. He fiddled with his blanket anxiously, his blue T-shirt too big for him, a hand-me-down from Thanh. He didn't like his brothers arguing, Anh knew, anxious about having to pick a side and vexing one or the other. Of all her siblings, Anh worried about Dao the most. She worried about life for him in America, that his shyness would make it hard for him to make friends once there. She had spent the past few months trying to break open his shell, encouraging him to play Đánh bi or Đánh đáo with the other children of the village by the banyan tree. "No, please," he would say, half hiding behind her. "I'd rather stay with you." Their mum pulled him up from his bed, his hands outstretched and holding on to hers. "Come on, Dao," she said as she picked him up. "Your brothers need to finish packing." Together they left the brothers' bedroom, and as they passed Anh's, the mum said, "Are you done? I could use your help with dinner."

"Yes, Ma," Anh said, stuffing her backpack with the remaining pieces of clothing spread out on her bed. She followed them into the adjacent kitchen, and her mother dropped Dao off her arms. "Can I help, too?" he asked. His mother gently brushed the hair off his face and said, "No, there's no tasks for little boys tonight. You can go in the living room with your father." He nodded, disappointed, and after glancing at Anh with his round eyes, he went up to the living room. Anh suspected that her mother had wanted a moment alone with her in the kitchen, to treasure an instant with her eldest daughter before her leaving.

Her baby brother, Hoang, was asleep in his cot, lulled by the rhythmic sounds of his mother's cooking, clinking pans and simmering oils. Anh stirred the pork as her mother chopped the fermented cabbage into small chunks, a tremble in her hand. It was as if they were acting a scene, a normal midweek evening, the kitchen their stage and their pots and pans their props. But as the two of them moved around the small space, they avoided each other's gaze, their usual chatter reduced to the occasional instruction,

"Make sure you get the scraps at the bottom of the pan" and "Add a bit of nước chấm." At several instances, Anh could see her mother opening her lips as if to speak, as if to let out a thought that had been weighing on her, but only sighs would come out.

Her younger sisters, Mai and Van, were setting the table, carefully juggling stacks of bowls and plates in their small hands, their long hair flowing behind them, the tap of their bare feet scarcely audible. While doing so, they revised their school lessons of the day. "Four times four, sixteen, four times five, twenty, four times six, twenty-four," they recited in a singsongy voice, one of them making the occasional mistake, the other one telling her off for it. "Twenty-*eight*, not twenty-*six*," Van said to Mai as they made their way back to the kitchen. Anh plated up the pork, steam rising from the pan, and handed them each a dish. They liked bringing the food to the table because they could snatch a few bits along the way, crumbs on their white vests giving them away. Sure enough, once they were out of sight, Anh heard Mai say, "That's too big a piece," while Van shushed her.

At the back of the living room, her father sat by the home altar, his back hunched, while Dao watched him attentively from the worn-out leather sofa. The altar was adorned with framed photos of their grandparents. There were Ông nội and Bà nội standing in front of their house and looking sternly at the camera, a newborn Van in their arms. In the background was their neighbor's chicken roaming on Vung Tham's dry and dark soil, their laundry hanging between their kitchen window and the nearby palm tree. There was Bà ngoại, posing by an ornate staircase at her daughter's wedding, small heels on her feet and her hair in a bun. And there was Ông ngoại, looking like an old Hollywood star in his close-up portrait, his white teeth showing and his hair barely gray. The four of them had died successively in the last three years, after Saigon had fallen and the last soldiers had gone back to America, like a gust of wind rippling through waning leaves. By then, they were old and weary, and their deaths hadn't come as a surprise. But the rapid pace made Anh wonder if the war had had something to do with it, if hope could be a source of life and its vanishing a foretelling of death.

With the back of his sleeve, Anh's father wiped the dust off the portrait of his mother, inspecting the frame by the candlelight. Once he was satisfied with its cleanness, he put it down carefully next to the others and lit some incense. He held the burning stick in his hands as he prayed, and soon her mother emerged from the kitchen to join him. She struck a match and lit the incense with it, and as they prayed together Anh heard them murmuring her name alongside those of Thanh and Minh, pleading for safe travels and calm seas. Dao stood up from the sofa and approached them, pulling on his mother's shirt. "Can I have one, too?" he asked, and she handed him her incense stick, lighting another one for herself. Anh watched as his timid voice joined his parents' prayers, the three of them on their knees, their ancestors watching over them. After a few minutes, her father stood up, clasping his hands. "Time for dinner," he said.

Dinner, she would remember. The moonlight illuminating the room with its soft glow, the smoke of the steamed cabbage and incense mingling together. Baby Hoang's small snores emerging from his cot, and their mother occasionally leaving her seat to check on him as he drifted in and out of sleep. The table, which was normally a place for raucous laughter and shouting, was instead shrouded in a nervous stillness. Their father's worn-out eyes looked down at his watch every few minutes. Their mother cut Dao's meat into smaller pieces, telling him it was time he learned how to use chopsticks properly. "You're not a baby anymore," she said, as he hung his head in embarrassment. "It's okay," Thanh whispered to him. "Sometimes I struggle with the big pieces of meat, too." Mai and Van, usually bursting with stories of their day at school, pushed the food around their plates, leaving it uneaten. Though they weren't exactly sure what was at stake, something about their parents' tense movements informed them that this was an unusual and somber evening.

To break the silence, Anh asked her father to repeat the plan one last time, and Minh let out a moan. *"Again? We all know it by heart already."* It was true. The plan was a simple one that her father had told them countless times, that she recited each night to herself before falling asleep, like she was studying for a test. She, Thanh, and Minh were to leave tonight for Da Nang, where a boat would be waiting to take them to Hong Kong. "There, you'll spend some time at a camp for people like us," her father said as Dao tried to operate his chopsticks the best he could, pieces of meat falling halfway between his mouth and his bowl. Her sisters had their elbows on the table, heads leaning on their hands, bored by this tale they had heard myriad times. He had already taken care of the payment to the boatmaster, twelve pieces of gold for each of them. "So you don't need to worry about that," her father said. "The rest of us will join you at the camp in a few weeks, and together we'll leave for America and meet Uncle Nam in *New Haven*."

He always explained the plan without a hint of a doubt in his voice, and Anh wondered if he had been masking his worries or if his conviction was real. She looked at him as he described the journey once more, in between sparse mouthfuls of pork and rice, his fingers drawing a map on the table. It hadn't occurred to her to question his authority or how much he really knew. It hadn't occurred to her that his brother and the smugglers may have fed him lies, omitting to mention the towering numbers of risks involved. Before the end of the war, her Uncle Nam had gone on the same journey with his wife and two children, sparking in her father the desire to leave Vietnam. Soon the spark grew into a wildfire, fed by each letter Nam sent, adorned with a stamp of the American flag and detailing his lavish new life of giant supermarkets and Fords and Chevrolets. The idea had become an obsession, deafening him to the concerns of their mother and blinding him to the hardships that surrounded the journey.

Because Anh, Minh, and Thanh were the three oldest children, their parents decided that they would travel ahead on a separate boat, dividing the family in two. It hadn't occurred to Anh that this breaking in half was the first sign of peril, the first clue that her father knew that one of the halves might fall.

Once dusk had settled, Anh kissed Hoang's forehead and hugged Mai and Van and Dao goodbye, all barely awake and longing for bed. She wished she could hold on to them longer, that she could squeeze them so tightly that a piece of their soul entered her heart. But she knew that there was a long night ahead, that the boat wouldn't wait for them in Da Nang, so she let go and turned to her mother. "Look after your brothers," she told her, handing Anh three lunch boxes containing the rest of the meal. Into her other hand, she slipped a small family photo taken by their neighbor the previous Tết. Anh took the photograph and examined their stern expressions. They were all sitting tightly packed together on their living room sofa and dressed in their best áo dais, Mai and Van and Anh in matching pink and the boys in pale blue. Their parents were on opposite ends, their mother heavily pregnant with Hoang. Mai and Van sat on their laps while Dao was on

Anh's at the center of the photograph, shifting his head so as not to hide hers. Thanh and Minh were at their sides, arms around their younger sisters. They had been trying hard to obey their father's pleas not to move or blink, unable to afford a second shot. Anh stared at each of their faces intensively, afraid that if her focus waned she would cry. "We'll see you in a few weeks," said her mom, as Anh looked away from the photograph and placed it in her backpack.

She gave her parents a final embrace and waited for Thanh and Minh to do the same. She would remember the stoic demeanor they had each adopted, how she had thought that any show of emotion would render them unable to let go of one another. "Always stick together no matter what," her father said, and she heard the urgency in his voice, that this was not an instruction but an order. He gave Minh a final pat on the shoulder and gently rubbed Thanh's hair, looking at his two oldest sons as if he were seeing them for the first time, taking in their features, engraving them in his mind. "Be good to your sister."

Dao grabbed their mother's arms as he sucked his thumb, and Mai let out a small yawn while waving a timid goodbye. "Are you scared?" Van asked Anh, looking out at the night that awaited her three older siblings with apprehension and distrust, scarce stars watching over their village, the leaves of the trees dancing slowly in the wind to the crickets' chirp. "It's so dark outside." Anh hesitated for a moment. "I'm not," she said. "Everything will be alright, you'll see." And she would always regret that her last utterance to her family had been a lie, false and useless words of reassurance. After a final nod to her parents, she took hold of Thanh and Minh's hands, and together they left their home and walked along the dusty road, headed north. Their family watched the three eldest children go, until the darkness of the night swallowed them completely and only the shadows of Vung Tham remained.

Three months later, Anh stood on a beach on the south coast of Hong Kong, her feet hot on the sand despite the early morning's breeze, the officer's intrusive yet reassuring hand on her shoulder. A doctor peeled back the sheets covering the bodies lying in front of them, one by one. She scanned the faces that revealed themselves underneath, aligned neatly on the sand, until she fell on those of her parents and siblings. She confirmed to the officer and doctor that they belonged to them. Sometimes, later in her life, she became resentful that they had fished them out at all; the absence of bodies had meant infinite possibilities, the possibility of life, of reunification and bliss.

2

Dao

The boat was crowded and reeking. I was sitting on my father's lap. Droplets of the sea had landed in my eyes and made them itch; my clothes were wet and sticking to my skin and making me cold. My sisters were on either side of my mother, clutching her arms as she held baby Hoang to her chest.

We'd left Vung Tham four days before in the pitch-black night and started on the long walk north. By the time we reached the coast of Da Nang the next evening, our feet were bleeding and covered in blisters, so much so that we tainted the boat red as we stepped into it.

Of course, I'd heard ghost stories back when I was alive.

There was the ghost of Ông ngoại, my grandfather,

for whom we left mangosteen

and cigarettes

next to his portrait and burning incense on the altar at home.

There was Thần làng, the village ghost, whose dripping clothes could still be heard

by children playing near the shore of the lake

that had swallowed him whole

a century prior.

But I always pictured ghosts as old, wise, playful souls, with lengthy beards and wrinkly skin. It hadn't occurred to me that there could be seven-year-old ghosts,

and yet, here I am.

I don't recall much about my death. There had been a storm the night before; the crashing waves rocked the boat and stiffened the baby's cries. I remember the next day, the boatmaster told us that we had drifted off course toward the south, and that it would take an extra day to reach Hainan.

I remember fishermen,

speaking a foreign tongue,

the blades of their knives glistening

in the dawn's sunlight.

Next, there was weightlessness. As I left my body and
gravity left me, I drifted on an ocean of white that was
surrounding me, until I was joined by my little brother and
father, and by my sisters and mother. Then, the whiteness
dissolved like fog when it sees the daylight approaching,

and I could see the boat from above,

except now it was sunk beneath the waves,

and bodies were floating all around it.

3

December 1978—South China Sea

Anh, Thanh, and Minh drifted onto the southern coast of Hainan eight days after leaving Vung Tham, with hollowed cheeks and sunken eyes, their clothes ragged and drenched by the previous day's storm. Minh's arm was bleeding from being thrown around in the rough seas, and Anh had fashioned a bandage for him from a T-shirt. She stepped off the boat with the thirty other passengers and took a few disoriented strides before lying down on the warm sand to try to stop her shivering. As her brothers joined her and the sun grazed her face, she saw the palm trees lining the coast, the calm, blue water that had nearly ended them only the night before. White cliffs and mountains covered with greenery dotted the skyline, and she realized that they had landed in a place of beauty. "I had no idea China looked like this," said Minh.

A dozen villagers arrived from inland, carrying flasks

and construction tools. They ran to the boatmaster, who gave them a pouch of what Anh assumed was gold coins. In return some of them went up to the boat to repair the damage, while others handed out water to the passengers. Anh noticed an old woman standing outside a house, observing the three of them from afar. She looked at them kindly, and Anh imagined how they must have seemed to her, huddled and shaking, their clothes torn and their eyes red from the seawater. She raised herself up to sit on the sand, straightening her back into a dignified posture, but by the time she looked again, the woman was gone.

Later, Anh was dozing off until a gentle tap on her shoulder woke her. The old woman was standing above her with a bowl of rambutans, handing it to her with the same compassionate look on her face. She uttered words that Anh couldn't understand, and it sank in that she and her brothers had made it, that they were now on foreign land and farther from home than they had ever been. As the men and passengers worked on repairing the boat, the first hints of homesickness slithered in her like venomous snakes. Her brothers sat on the sand eating the fruit, juice trickling onto their chins. Anh took their family photo carefully out of her backpack. Water had filtered through the paper and half of the ink was gone, her and her brothers' faces along with it, each replaced by white and yellow streaks that ran across the image. Her parents and Mai and Van were barely visible beneath the black blotches that peppered what remained of it. She stared at their disfigured features in a daze, as if their faces would reappear, before placing the soggy image inside her bag, making sure not to bend any of its edges.

By the time they'd finished eating, the repairs were complete, and the captain was rushing everyone back to the boat, wanting to take advantage of the good weather. Around Anh, the passengers rose from the sand, their sense of hope renewed, the worst now behind them. She saw fathers lifting their sleeping children and carrying them, a mother humming a lullaby while nursing her baby with the little milk she had left. Anh and her brothers got up, and as she boarded, Anh looked in vain for the stranger who had showed them kindness. With regret, she left without saying goodbye.

They reached the Hong Kong shore two days later, their rotting and cracked boat gracelessly crashing onto the southern coast of Lantau Island. A police boat made its way to them, the officers on board shouting. "Where do you come from?" they asked the boatmaster. They spoke English, which Anh could partially grasp, her father having taught English in Vung Tham. After a few exchanges, the policemen checked on the passengers, first aid kits in hand. One of them unwrapped Minh's bandage, neither cold nor friendly, and laid an ointment on his cut, which made Minh grimace with pain. The officer put small ban-

dages on it and gave the siblings some dry biscuits and a
carton of milk, which they gulped down.

They were ushered onto a bus and transported to a massive
dockyard, covered with high beams and a tattered, gray tarp
roof, the sky filtering through its holes. Anh was engulfed
by the stench of sweat and filth and the masses of people
it contained. She found herself shivering again, the dampness and coldness of the place invading her bones. Stationed
densely on the floor were men and women of all ages, lying
on makeshift mattresses. Some were sleeping; others played
cards and looked up at the sound of the newcomers. Doctors roamed around the dockyard, checking the lungs and
mouths of the lodgers. Clothing rails hung in between the
metal pillars present across the room, drenched clothes dan-
gling from them, splashes of water droplets falling to the
floor in a symphonic rhythm. There must have been more
than a hundred people, and yet silence loomed heavily, each
of the siblings' steps echoing through the hollow space. A
police officer shouted at them in Cantonese. He pointed to a
corner, repeating the words, elongating each one as if slow-
ing down would help them understand, and when still none
of them moved but simply stared back at him, frightened,
he rolled his eyes and ushered them toward a wall at the
back of the building.

There, they found a worn-out mattress waiting for them,
and Anh dropped her bag onto it. Nearby was a family
of four, the father holding the youngest in his arms while

the mother sobbed, her daughter quietly stroking her hair. On the other side of the siblings was a young man in his early thirties. He watched them while they settled on their mattress and took in their new surroundings. Anh could sense him observing their nervous movements, the way they slowly patted down the futon and sat on its edges. The officer came back again, shouting words at her she could not understand.

"He's asking where you've traveled from," said the young man next to her. Anh turned to him. She noticed a large scar on his forehead and eyebrow, slashing it in two.

"Vung Tham," she said. "In South Central Vietnam."

The man translated for her as the officer nodded and then left, scribbling something on a sheet of paper.

"You speak Cantonese?" Minh asked, and the man laughed. "Of course. Lots of us do. We're Hoa people."

"Where are we?" asked Anh, trying to conceal her fear.

"We're in quarantine," he said. "You'll be kept here for two weeks. And after that, who knows."

The four of them fell silent, the brothers looking up at Anh expectantly, like soldiers awaiting their next order. But she, too, was unsure of what to do with this new information. Their parents had not told her about this part, about dockyards and traces of feces on mattresses, how deafening the collective silence of a crowd is. She looked at the people around her and realized that she had become one of them, that she was homeless and smelling and weak, a carrier of disease, that she was now perceived as vermin. A woman came up to them and sprayed their hair with a white powder that made them cough.

"For de-licing," she said, already moving on to the next group of newcomers.

"No need to look so sad," the young man said, seeing Anh's, Thanh's, and Minh's morbid expressions. "Consider yourself lucky you made it. Sometimes they don't even let our boats dock." He scratched his hair, dandruff falling out of it.

"What happens if they don't?" asked Thanh in his high-pitched voice. The man shrugged, looking away.

"They have to go all the way back to Vietnam."

Anh stared at a yellow stain in the corner of the mattress. The man looked to the children once more, this time with more compassion, a faint smile forming.

"You'll be fine," he said. "Just make sure you don't cough in front of the officers. And, if you feel unwell, do this when you see them approach."

He pinched his cheeks, and they flushed to a healthy rose. Anh wasn't sure whether to nod or laugh, if this was a joke or a matter of life and death. The mother on Anh's left let out a loud, piercing cry. They all turned to stare at her. The daughter continued to caress her hair, and her husband shushed her nervously, his eyes alert and shifting left to right.

"Why is she crying?" Thanh asked the man, whose rosy cheeks were beginning to fade.

The man looked uneasy. "Their baby died last night," he said. He looked down, his fingers fidgeting. He swiveled on his mattress, turning his back to the children, their conversation over.

Minh shifted closer to Anh and whispered in her ear so that Thanh wouldn't hear. "What if they don't let Ma and Dad's boat in?"

She grabbed his arm, checking how his wound was healing underneath the bandages.

"They will," she said. And after a pause she said it again, more to herself than her brother. "They will."

Minh didn't question her assertion, perhaps because he had gotten the answer he wanted, the reasoning irrelevant. They surveyed the scene in the warehouse, the mother still sobbing, policemen patrolling the grounds, shouting the occasional foreign word. Another officer approached them, this one more kindly. He carried with him a pile of clothes and handed them to Anh. "Here," he said. "To keep you warm."

"Thank you," whispered Anh, taking the clothes. There was a suit jacket that she put on Minh's shoulders, an itchy sweater she gave to Thanh.

"We should try and sleep," she said, putting on a gray cardigan. "We didn't sleep much on the boat."

Anh saw the dread in her brothers, that they, too, wondered how they would be able to live in this dockyard for the next two weeks—their senses assaulted by its dilapidated state—as they waited for their parents and siblings. Thanh rested his head on Anh's rumbling stomach while Minh wrapped his hands tightly around her arm. Before long they had all passed out, asleep.

4

Koh Kra Island, Thailand, November 22, 1979

VIETNAMESE REFUGEES RESCUED FROM THAI ISLAND

BY JACK BARNES, SENIOR REPORTER

Reports came in that 17 Vietnamese refugees, some of them children, were murdered by fishermen on the island of Koh Kra in the Gulf of Thailand. Allegedly, 500 Thai fishermen were involved in the rape of 37 women on Koh Kra over the course of 22 days that month. The women came from four different boats and were brought to Koh Kra Island by the fishermen, who rammed their boats against the refugees to prevent escape. They grabbed the women and girls they considered the most attractive off the sinking boats and kidnapped them onto their own. The rest of the passengers were left at sea, to be engulfed by waves, though the men often attempted to rescue their wives and daughters, some drowning in the process. The abducted women were then brought to Koh Kra, their boat nudging against the bodies of men, women, and children that floated near the shore.

Some women found caves in which they hid, waist-deep in water, the flesh on their legs ravaged by crabs. One survivor asserted that she witnessed a fisherman setting fire to a bush, and saw the women hiding there run away, screaming and on fire.

The most attractive women were taken off the island by the fishermen and later sold to brothels in southern Thailand or forced to travel with them and traded between boats.

After 22 days on this hellish island, the 156 surviving women, the youngest amongst them 12 years old, were rescued by a UNHCR boat. They were brought to Songkhla refugee camp in southern Thailand. The police held seven fishermen as suspects. When asked about Koh Kra by the officials, the women recalled that men came on and off the island during their captivity, using their bodies day and night.

A worker from Songkhla refugee camp later disclosed that an overwhelming majority of the women in the refugee camp between the ages of 10 and 50 years old had been victims of sexual assault.

5

December 1978—Hong Kong

"Say aah," the doctor said, poking a stick at the back of Minh's mouth.

Minh obliged but couldn't help gagging. The doctor scribbled notes on his form and without a word nor glance moved on to the next family.

They had been in the dockyard for two weeks now. Fourteen days of sickness and dampness and filth, of policemen questioning them and doctors inspecting them every day like cattle. The young man and the family that was next to them on their arrival had now gone, replaced by a young couple and a mother and son not yet used to their new surroundings, their hair and skin still holding the sea's salt.

"When are they going to pick us up?" Minh asked Anh as he got up to stretch his back.

Today, it was their turn. They had passed all the medical tests, suppressed their coughs, and obeyed the policemen's growling orders swiftly; they had eaten the bowls of cold and undercooked rice given to them without complaints. But as they reached their final day in quarantine, Anh sensed that if she spent a minute more breathing the dockyard's air, she might explode into a thousand pieces.

"I think they usually come in the afternoon. Be patient," she told Minh.

Thanh was dosing off at the edge of the mattress, thinner than he was a month ago, when their journey had yet to begin. Anh observed his feeble frame, his belly growing and shrinking with his breathing, and she wondered how long it would take for him to disappear completely, until only his bones remained. A voice she had never heard before interrupted her grim thoughts.

"Anh, Thanh, and Minh?" the voice asked.

Anh looked up at the woman and quickly got up, nudging Thanh to do the same.

"Yes," she said. "That's us."

The woman smiled. "I'm Isabel," she said. "I'm here to take you to Kai Tak, the camp where you'll be staying for now. Can you please pack all your belongings?"

"Yes," Anh said. "Yes, we'll do that right now."

Isabel smiled again. "Good. I'll be right back," she said, making her way to another nearby group that had arrived at the same time as the siblings.

"Are we leaving?" Thanh asked. "For real?"

"Yes," said Minh, shuffling his tattered clothes into his backpack. "Hurry up and pack your stuff."

The daylight blinded them as they followed Isabel out of the dockyard, along with a dozen other refugees. Anh took a deep breath and inhaled the outside air she hadn't breathed in fourteen days, an air that smelled of gasoline and the sea.

"Come on," said Isabel, giving Anh a gentle tap on her back. "The bus is just on the left of the harbor."

The camp sat near Hong Kong International Airport, an hour's drive from the dockyard. As they stepped off the bus, they were welcomed by the sight of a towering metal gate and two armed men guarding it, their eyes following the newcomers as they entered the site. Anh had no idea what to expect. Her father's plan did not include inside the camp, only how to get there. So, when she passed through the gates, Thanh and Minh closely behind her, she was relieved to see a world far less sinister looking than the dockyard. White, squared huts with metal roofs lined the ground, a brown similar to Vung Tham's earth. Refugees shuffled in between the huts and the roads, carrying their children or buckets of water, and she heard them speaking Vietnamese, Southern and Northern accents mingling together. "It looks *huge*," said Thanh.

Isabel brought them inside one of the white huts, and Anh was surprised by its vastness, unimaginable from the outside. It contained rows of three-tiered bunk beds with curtains attached to give a semblance of privacy, the top ones only a few inches from the ceiling. About twenty other refugees were already in the hut, looking suspiciously at the siblings as they made their way into their new housing. There were children their age and grandmas and grandpas, young men and women and pregnant mothers. As in the dockyard, the smell of grime and perspiration was there, too, perhaps to a lesser extent but enough to make Anh grimace slightly as she walked into the room.

"Here," Isabel said. "You'll be on this top bunk. You'll have to share one for now."

"Our parents and siblings are coming soon," said Anh. "They'll be here in the next two week or so." Isabel turned to look at her anew, as if only realizing now that she was only a child.

"That's good," she said. "Once they're here, you can all be in the same hut together. And we'll have you come into the resettlement office for an interview as well, so we can learn more about you."

With no other choice, the three siblings adapted quickly to their new life in the North camp of Kai Tak. Instead of the sound of boats approaching shore that they had grown accustomed to in the dockyard, the roar of landing and departing planes now punctuated their days, leaving white trails in the sky that slowly merged with clouds. As their first weeks there passed, a routine soon established itself. Each day, they woke up at eight in the bunk bed they shared. They put on their clothes alongside their dormmates, trying to hide their bodies as best they could, and ate a piece of fruit for breakfast, oranges or longans or bananas.

Then, they would rush to their English lessons, where they were all taught by Mrs. Jones, who spoke with a strong English accent, one that Anh would later realize was "posh." The classroom looked surprisingly similar to the one they had in Vung Tham—white walls covered in children's drawings, a big, dusty chalkboard, and small wooden desks. They were placed in the intermediate class, where they recited phrases like "I have two siblings" and "The weather looks gray today" and "I am going to the market to buy some fish," sentences that they would repeat to one another in the night, chuckling at the foreignness coming from their lips. Thanh's accent was the best out of the three, his tongue still flexible enough to adjust to the new language, while Minh and Anh still struggled with the *r*'s and the *s*'s and the *z*'s.

They joined the line for lunch at noon, carrying their red, plastic bowls with them. The meal was often a bland and lukewarm bowl of congee with a few vegetables, soft food fit for the teeth of babies and elders. "Are we going to have to eat this every day?" Minh had asked during their first meal, watching the mushy rice slide off from his spoon. "Yes," Anh whispered. "Please stop complaining; people can hear you."

The UN High Commission for Refugees oversaw the camp, and fieldworkers like Isabel from the Red Cross, and the Salvation Army and Save the Children roamed the grounds all day, first aid kits or checklists in their hands. Watching the fieldworkers, Anh soon understood that the camp was a state of limbo, a purgatory between their old and new lives. Now and then, United Nations officials from the Resettlement Office would call in a particular family or group and tell them that a country had agreed to welcome them onto their soil. All the camp's residents would look on, holding their breath as their neighbors made the short walk from their hut to the one that housed the officials who would decide their fate.

As they left the office, some burst out in elation, kneeling on the floor in prayer, their arms motioning up and down while they muttered their thanks and the names of deceased loved ones. Others would emerge with the color drained from their faces, trying hard not to break down in tears, which meant that the country they would now call home was one they either didn't know or didn't want.

Resettlement was a lottery, and there were winners and losers. The United States was the Holy Grail of destinations, the Land of the Free, of cowboys and Elvis, and most of the refugees spent their days dreaming of a life there, of becoming businessmen and restaurant owners, of generating a lineage of doctors and engineers. Germany or Italy were the consolation prizes, countries that seemed so foreign to them and whose languages they could not speak; countries that meant grieving a whole life they had already imagined and that they had longed for, a life they had told their children about as bedtime stories and that they had dreamed of in their own beds. Anh was no different: as soon as she arrived at the camp, she had started fantasizing about beginning life from scratch in the Land of the Free or, as their father used to say at the dinner table in Vung Tham, with a twinkle in his eye, to start living their *American dream*.

As the siblings gradually grew accustomed to camp life, the majority of their days were spent waiting for their family. At the sound of a bus approaching, Thanh and Minh would rush to the wired gate, Anh trying to calm their pace but equally eager to go. Each time, they would scan the faces of the passengers as they descended from the vehicle, and each time, they would be disappointed when none belonged to their family, walking back to their hut defeated. Three weeks went by, and their parents and siblings were still nowhere to be seen. "When are they coming?" Thanh asked constantly. "Soon," Anh answered. "Any day now." Yet as each hour passed, the sinking feeling that something was not right grew in her stomach. Part of her didn't want to act on it; part of her thought that as long as the three of them kept going about their days nothing bad could happen, that bringing up her family's absence would only serve to make it real. But after a month, the suspicion grew too large for her to contain on her own, and she went to Isabel's office after lunch, while her brothers were at school. "The rest of my family is still not here," she told Isabel. "They should have arrived by now."

Isabel looked up at her, calm and composed, as if she had heard those words many times before. "Can you describe them to me, please?" she said, grabbing a piece of paper.

Anh told her about her father's towering height and strong build, her mother's beauty mark, like a shadow permanently resting above her right eye. She told her about Mai's and Van's dark, wavy chest-length hair, Dao's tiny purple birthmark on his left knee, Hoang's feeble infant frame.

Isabel scribbled notes, her pen gliding smoothly on the page. "Don't worry," she said as she opened the door for Anh. "I'm sure they'll be here very soon."

In January the temperature dropped, and the camp grew busier. Anh was washing her brothers' clothes outside their hut when she saw Isabel running toward her.

"Anh," she said. "Can you come with me, please? Now."

Anh could tell by her agitated voice and hurried pace that something wasn't right, though she could not comprehend what was about to come. She went back to Isabel's office, where a man was sitting in the same chair that she had occupied only a week prior, the chair in which she had so precisely and lovingly described her parents and siblings to Isabel. The man introduced himself to her and shook her hand while Isabel translated his Cantonese. "He's a marine officer," she said. "They have found some . . . bodies on the beach, some of them matching the descriptions you gave me of your family and their belongings."

The rest happened in a haze. Isabel had crouched down and was holding Anh's arms, looking straight into her eyes. Anh felt the urge to throw up, this morning's congee making its way back to her throat. "You don't have to," Isabel was saying. "You don't have to." But no, she had to; she had to identify the bodies. The unknown would be worse, she thought, so much worse than the sight. Her hands were weak in Isabel's palms. She shook her head. "I need to see them," Anh said.

They traveled with the officer to a beach on the southern coast, along with other camp residents who had missing family members, the sun beating down on them in the sweltering heat. The doctor pulled back the sheets, each concealing a body, of which two adults and three children and one infant stood out to Anh, their faces so familiar and yet so alien, now that they no longer contained life.

They were buried in a gravesite near Kai Tak, alongside other Vietnamese who hadn't made it safely to shore. Anh and her brothers looked on from afar as the graves were dug and the coffins lowered into them. They refused to come nearer, even as Isabel ushered them forward. "Are you sure you don't want to say goodbye?" she asked, but they shook their heads. They wanted the memory of that moment to be a blur, something indistinct that they would never be able to recount clearly in their minds, that would degrade over time like the photograph in Anh's bag.

Their parents' and siblings' names were engraved on

a wooden plaque that hung in the prayer room. Next to it was another plaque and next to that was another, rows of etched plaques that covered the walls floor to ceiling with names of deceased Vietnamese. Anh thought how easily her name could have ended up on that wall, too, how it could have been her instead of her brothers and sisters.

After the burial, Isabel drove them back to the camp, glancing nervously at the three of them in the rearview mirror. Anh's brothers stared out of the windows on either side, their sniffles audible. It began to register for Anh that she was now the eldest of their small family of three. Her brothers were her sole responsibility and burden. She held their lives in her bony fingers.

"You'll need to wash your hands when we get back," she told them, imagining this is what her mother would have said.

6

Thanh and Minh were playing soccer with the neighbors' children, weaving the ball silkily between the iron huts and the bystanders. Every afternoon, their shrieks and cheers reverberated throughout the camp as they kicked the ball to one another, makeshift goalposts outlined by empty bottles of water. Anh looked on anxiously, afraid her brothers would get hurt. The mothers often watched the games alongside her and had taken her under their wing. They made sure she never strayed too far from their quarters into the more fearsome neighborhoods of Kai Tak or used the shower facilities alone, and they disciplined her brothers on her behalf when her voice wasn't stern enough.

The camp had become Anh and her brothers' own little world, a miniature version of Vietnam. Although ten thousand people lived in it, few wandered far from their huts, and soon faces became friendly, names were exchanged, and conversations sparked up. Isabel allowed Anh day passes to go work at a garment factory outside the camp, where she made fifty Hong Kong dollars a day, three times a week. While her brothers were at school studying math or geography or arts and crafts, she took the dilapidated bus with her fellow workers to the vast, cold warehouse near the southern coast of Lantau Island. She came home long after their classes were over for the day but didn't like leaving them alone. She imagined Thanh and Minh drifting around, shadowy figures luring them into harm. She worried that she would come back one day, and Isabel would be waiting for her by the gate with her head lowered, the coroner Anh remembered so well standing by her side again.

However, they needed money: the food they were given by the camp not enough for their growing bodies. The hours were long and the pay was low, but it allowed Anh to buy extra vegetables and fruit from the grocery store, and bánh cuốn from the Vietnamese hawker's stall near their hut, to make their lives a little more like they had been at home. The hawker came from a village not far from theirs, and her food resembled the dishes their mother used to make. One bite and memories of Vung Tham flooded back: returning from school and hearing the thump of their mother's knife as it minced pork and wood-ear mushrooms, kissing her hello and gathering at the dining table to begin their homework, math or French or science. And so, Anh left her brothers behind, instructing them to walk straight from school back to their hut, asking other mothers to keep watch over them, and they obliged, happily eagle-eyed.

Her mother had taught her how to sew, whole Saturday mornings spent with her and Bà ngoại at the dinner table, embroidering small scraps of fabric from her siblings' tattered clothes. They sewed loose buttons or stitched the rips in her brothers' shirts while discussing the latest village gossip, often stories of marital troubles she was still too young to fully understand—a neighbor's wandering eye or a friend of a friend's daughter pregnant out of wedlock. With that leisurely experience on hand, Anh thought the job would be easy. But on her first day, she witnessed the pace at which everyone worked and realized she had been wrong. For weeks her hands bled from the pricks she inflicted on herself by sewing at a speed beyond her competency, the other seamstresses barely acknowledging her presence, their aloofness pervasive, their lunch breaks taken in silence at each corner of the large room. They all knew they could be fired in the blink of an eye, how easily someone more efficient could replace them, the cutthroat nature of their employment reflected in their behavior.

Anh worried that she would never be good enough for this job, and that if she wasn't good enough for this, she would never be good enough for any job. She panicked, thinking that she would never manage on her own, without her mother guiding her. But she wasn't on her own; she had her brothers to look after, and they depended on her. If not for herself, she had to try for them, and so she carried on, until soon enough she could sew tablecloths and curtains, T-shirts and trousers, at the same speed as the seamstresses who had been there for years.

By the time Anh took the bus back to Kai Tak, it was dark. She liked to wipe her sleeve on the window and admire the city through the mist; streetlights and speeding motorbikes, drunken passersby and weary businessmen hurrying back home. It was a sight so different from Vung Tham, so alive and bustling it was like watching a film, her window a screen. The city surrounded her, and still it felt distant and out of reach, a whole world that she could see yet not grasp, the camp and the factory the only two places unlocked to her. She returned to the hut exhausted at the end of the day and with cramps in her hands, her brothers drowsy and getting ready for bed.

"How was your day?" she would ask them. Often, Minh would just shrug and say, "Good," while Thanh would exclaim, "Look what I did today," rushing to show her his latest papier-mâché bowl or colored world map, proud of his day's work. They wouldn't think to ask her how her day was. She was now their North Star, the most solid presence in their lives, and so of course she had to be fine, and she wanted them to assume that she was, too.

The deaths of their family had become a forbidden subject, deflected at all costs, as if mentioning it would result in a hex being cast on them. But still the memory loomed above

Anh's head as a constant cloud, invading her thoughts and keeping her awake at night, the swollen, dormant faces of her family flashing before her. On the outside, she tried hard to remain composed, to be the calm eye in the whirling cyclone of her brothers' lives.

She could see her brothers struggling with their grief, but being younger, theirs took the shape of sporadic fits and cries. Thanh would erupt at the smallest of predicaments, a too-cold dinner or a soccer defeat that resulted in him hurling his fists at opponents. "It's not fair!" he would scream, and Anh would drag him away over the dusty pitch and back to their hut. Minh, in contrast, would stay quiet for hours on end, eyebrows furrowed and lips pursed, pacing in circles in front of their hut. "Why was Dad such an idiot? Of course, his plan wouldn't work," he would say, kicking the ground, hands in his pockets. Each time, Anh had to calm him down before he attracted the unwanted attention of their neighbors and the camp's fieldworkers. She could not comfort him, for that only made him angrier. Instead, she tried to distract him, asking him to run an errand for her or to help her wash their clothes, until his anger evaporated.

Above all, it was their uncle they were angry at. Even Anh, who tried hard to be compassionate and fair in her judgments, could not tame the flicker of resentment that grew within her, until he had become a villain in her mind. She blamed him for their misery, for putting the idea of leaving

Vung Tham in their father's head and breaking their family beyond repair. A few days after her parents and siblings had been laid into the ground and those thoughts began pervading Anh's mind, Isabel approached her, gently.

"You've been called in to do an initial interview with the Resettlement Office." She saw Anh's anxiety as she said these words. "Don't worry. They'll only ask you a few easy questions about you and your brothers, for your resettlement application." She gestured for Anh to follow her, and together they made their way to the Resettlement Office. Anh tried to take assured steps, to embody the head of the family she now was, as her father would have been.

"We're very sorry for your loss, Anh. My deepest condolences to you and your brothers," said the UN officer, Mr. Barnett, as he motioned for Anh to take a seat. "We want you to have the best lives possible."

Anh held her head low, keeping quiet, scared that sobs would escape as soon as she opened her mouth.

"You're the eldest of the family, and your brothers' guardian, so I'm going to ask you a few questions, if that's okay," the officer continued. "You told Isabel you wanted to go to America, correct? You speak a little English, right? Your father was a teacher during the war?"

Anh nodded mechanically, taking in the man's words, "eldest of the family," the eldest survivor.

"That's good. It helps if you speak English. Do you have any family abroad? It can help your application. If the American authorities know you have family there, they might be more willing to welcome you. You'll have sponsorship."

Anh didn't know what sponsorship was. She didn't know what she wanted besides having her family by her side, to have her father answer these questions in her stead. "Family abroad." She remembered what her father had told her, that once they arrived in New Haven, she would go work at her aunt's nail salon. At that moment, she was appalled by the idea. She didn't want to be a part of their lives, to see her cousins coming home from school, their mother hugging them hello, their father teaching them how to ride a bike, to be reminded of the pain he had caused them all. She hated the familial bliss she imagined they lived and that her uncle had taken from her. She believed she didn't need them. America would welcome them with or without her uncle's name on their application form, and once they arrived, they would make a life for themselves on their own. And so, after a brief pause in which Mr. Barnett looked at her attentively, pen hovering above his form, she said, "No. It's just us."

The officer ticked a box on the form, not inquiring further.

"Okay, thank you. We'll find you a safe new country to call home," he said, standing up and shaking Anh's hand, then showing her the way out.

A month later, as she watched her brothers mingle with the other children on the soccer field, she still carried a nagging worry about whether she had been right to say, "It's just us," wondering if the box the officer had ticked would have any bearing on their resettlement in America. It had been an impulse, she realized, remnants of childish behavior. And now, she wondered if this impulse would have an aftermath.

"Goal!" screamed Thanh.

She clapped for her brother's feat, and the surrounding mothers turned to congratulate her.

*

After I learned about Koh Kra, I couldn't sleep for three days, and again I asked myself, *Why do I want to do this?*

I guess it is more of a need than a want.

I want to know everything.

I want to make this history vivid in my mind.

And as my knowledge and understanding grow, I feel a responsibility to pass it on, as if I'd inherited this story, as if it is now my burden and my care.

I cannot let it fade away; I cannot let it die.

7

August 2022—Koh Kra Island, Thailand

The water and the skies are clear blue. A motorboat approaches the island at full speed carrying an Australian couple and their three young children. They're accompanied by a guide. Four or five times a day, he brings tourists from the luxury resorts on the island of Ko Chang to snorkel in the reefs of nearby Koh Kra and its surrounding islets.

The parents watch their children marvel at the fish and coral as other families join them in their own boats. They make small talk, *Where-are-you-from-which-hotel-are-you-in-is-this-your-first-time-in-Thailand?* A boy nudges his parents to come look at the fish with him; another one is crying because he felt something bite his leg. The teenager complains the water is too cold, but after a minute or so, her whining turns to wonder as the ocean starts to reveal its secrets to them.

From their boat, the father notices what looks like the remains of an abandoned lighthouse on the western coast of the island. "Can we visit this?" he asks, but the guide shakes his head briskly. "No, no, it's forbidden. Too dangerous. Too old." The father doesn't insist, and instead he takes a photograph, his children laughing in the water in the foreground. Back at the hotel that evening, he will post it to his social feeds, Instagram, Facebook, Twitter—and caption it, "First time snorkeling!" basking in the likes he will receive from friends and relatives, the children slightly embarrassed by the unsolicited display of their private lives, their meager protests and pouts unnoticed as his eyes focus on the tiny screen.

When midday arrives, the guide gently prods the family to return to Ko Chang. Before starting the engine, he asks the children if they've had a good time, and they answer yes in unison. The parents acquiesce with a nod and a smile. At their hotel, they have an abundant and well-deserved lunch, tom yum and pad thai and chicken fingers and fries. The parents tan as their children play in the nearby pool, swimming bands on their arms, small waves forming as they splash about.

Inside the ruins of the lighthouse on Koh Kra, carefully shielded from tourists and unwanted visitors, are wooden beams that stretch from wall to wall. Although rotten and dented and covered with spiderwebs, some words in Vietnamese, coarsely scratched onto them, are still legible.

> *Women, find a hiding place right away.*
> *Cut your hair and pretend to be a boy.*

8

May 1979—Kai Tak Refugee Camp,
Hong Kong

"Can we get sodas, please?" Thanh asked on their weekly run to the camp's grocery store, a wooden structure run by one of the elderly inhabitants. Anh looked inside her wallet. She was still waiting to be paid for the week, and it contained only a handful of dollars.

"Just one, then. That you can share."

Minh grabbed a can of Coca-Cola and put it in their basket, next to the rice cakes and mangoes. "They're just like the ones the American soldiers used to drink when they came to our village," Thanh said.

The store owner scanned the Coca-Cola can, handing it to Minh before turning his attention to the rest of their groceries. "How's school?" he asked them. "Good," Thanh said. "I can count to a hundred in English now," and the grocer gave him a thumbs-up.

The sun began to fade into mist as they walked home, Anh and Minh ahead, Thanh lingering behind, kicking pebbles with his foot. Anh had turned around to tell him to hurry up when they suddenly heard a scream followed by a commotion as people ran toward it, women ushering their children out of the way. Violent quarrels in the camp were common. Squabbles between Northern Vietnamese, Southern Vietnamese, and Hoa people occurred daily, sometimes over diverging political beliefs, other times over meager trivialities, a cool glance or a shower that took too long. Anh had told her brothers to stay out of them, to run the other way if they ever heard a fight break out. But this time, perhaps because they were together or because there was something familiar in the screaming voice they had heard, curiosity got the better of her, and together they approached slowly, hoping to watch from afar.

His eyes were firmly shut, swollen and blue, his nose and lips a jumble of red, but there was no denying who lay on the ground. They instantly recognized the man they had stayed next to in the dockyard for two weeks, the one who had first told them about quarantine and camps, who recommended that they pinch their cheeks and suppress their coughs. His attackers had already scattered, and he lay unconscious on the muddy ground as two women tended to his wounds with damp towels. Thanh made to approach, but Anh held him by the shoulders. They stayed a few yards away, half hidden behind the wall of a hut, peeking from behind it.

"Do you think he's dead?" Minh whispered. She turned to look at him and saw that he was scared, that even though he had lived through a war and the death of his parents and siblings, he had never witnessed a violent death with his own eyes. Anh stayed quiet. She wasn't sure of the answer. Two paramedics appeared and took the man away on a stretcher, and Anh sensed this would be the last time they would ever see him, their last image of him being his fragile body lying in the dirt, lifeless.

"Come on," said Anh, looking away. "Let's go."

They continued their walk back to their hut, Thanh and Minh sipping their soda quietly, handing the can to one another after each sip, digesting what they had just seen.

"Anh!" Isabel shouted, running toward them as Anh was about to open the door to their hut. "Can you three go to the Resettlement Office now? Mr. Barnett needs to talk to you."

They dropped their groceries inside and hurried down to the office. Anh didn't know what to expect, the worst had already happened to them. She knocked and Mr. Barnett opened the door, a wide smile on his face. "Come in," he said.

The three of them sat down on the wooden chairs across from him, Thanh barely taller than the desk between them, Minh on the edge of his seat.

"I have some bad news and some good news," the officer said. "Bad news is that the United States wasn't able to accept your application. They're reducing their intake of refugees for the moment." He paused, awaiting the children's reaction, but they continued to stare with their alert eyes, and so he went on. "The good news is you'll be leaving for the United Kingdom in three weeks' time. They've accepted your application."

Instead of smiling back, Anh gripped the edge of her seat and bit her lip, confusion and anger rising in her as her breathing got tighter and tighter. The United Kingdom wasn't part of the plan. It wasn't in the life her parents had mapped out for them. Her mind racing, Anh remembered how she had refused to tell Mr. Barnett about her uncle in America. "No. It's just us," the sound of the pen gliding across the box on the form. Mr. Barnett continued to talk, but Anh couldn't listen. She barely noticed her brothers looking up at her bewildered, waiting for her to explain that there was a mistake, that their road was one that led to America and America only. She muttered a feeble thank you, got up from her chair, and left, her brothers following behind.

9

May 1979—Kai Tak Refugee Camp,
Hong Kong

Thanh sat on the ground in front of their hut, head resting in his palms. His brother and sister were inside packing their luggage, which wouldn't take long considering how few belongings they had left. Anh had managed to save up enough money to buy a small suitcase at the Red Cross shop. Their roommates were envious of this symbol of departure and new beginnings, and some watched with grudging looks on their faces as she unpacked the siblings' backpacks and filled the suitcase with their contents. Thanh had tried to help with the task, but as he dug his hand into Anh's backpack to empty it, he stumbled upon a crinkled piece of paper at the bottom. He pulled out the photograph of his family at their last Tết, sitting tightly together on their living room sofa, the colors now muddled and their expressions indiscernible. He looked intensely, trying to catch glimpses of their faces beneath the blotches, but to no avail. He tore the photograph to pieces, furious tears flooding his face, as their dormmates looked on, baffled.

"Why didn't you keep it dry?" he shouted at Anh, ripped scraps at his feet.

"We were in the middle of the ocean," she said, pleading, picking up the pieces, Minh coming to help her. "What on earth was I supposed to do?"

"You could have, if you had tried harder," he said, storming out of the hut before Anh had time to respond.

Deep down he knew she was right, that he had asked for the impossible. But still, he wanted to be angry. He wanted someone to blame for this last tangible memento of his family being ruined.

Tomorrow, they were going back to the dockyard to quarantine before leaving the country, as if Kai Tak was its own microbiome, more noxious than the rest of Hong Kong. He dreaded going back, the cold, foul air of misery that pervaded the vast space, the doctors checking his lungs and tonsils every day, digging a wooden stick down his throat that made him gag. And yet he was also relieved to have a little extra time on familiar ground, to not jump into the unknown quite so soon. They were due to leave for Bournemouth in two weeks by plane. "You'll be flying among the clouds," Mrs. Jones said, and the thought filled him with both dread and anticipation. They had said their farewells to their class that same morning with promises to keep in touch, even though none of them had addresses or phone numbers to exchange. The teacher had done her best to praise her country to him and his siblings once she'd discovered where they were being relocated to. "You'll be able to speak English there," she told him, "to put all the phrases I taught you to good use."

"Like 'The weather looks gray today,'" he said, wanting to show he remembered his lessons well.

"Yes," she laughed. "You'll need that one a lot."

She went on to say that maybe, if they behaved, they would be able to take a trip to London and see the queen at Buckingham Palace and her guards who wore fur hats and red suits and who stood still for hours on end. As she said this, she wiped tears from her face, her words unconvincing.

He had never seen his sister more distressed than after that fateful day in the Resettlement Office. Anh stayed quiet the length of the walk back to the hut and throughout dinner, as he and Minh asked endless questions to the hollowed shell she had become. They wondered aloud about their uncle and New Haven and asked, "What is Sopley?" and "Where is Sopley?" as she frowned into her bowl of congee. The next day, she woke them up early, earlier than usual, and rushed them out the door and back to the Resettlement Office. Three knocks on the door, "Come in," and there they were again, on the small wooden chairs. He expected to see Mr. Barnett behind the desk, but instead another officer, a woman he had only seen in passing, was sitting there. Anh tried to reason with her all the same, her voice timid and pleading, telling the stoic woman about their uncle in America, the life that awaited them in New Haven. But she glanced at the file in her hand and shook her head.

"It says here that you don't have any family abroad." She paused. "Look, they're just not accepting refugees from the camp at present, and you three need to leave." She sighed and looked at each of them in turn as they gazed up, pinning their hopes on her. Thanh could tell she regretted her earlier brusque tone as she adopted a softer one. "It's no good for you to stay here too long, with no parents . . . You understand? In England you'll be able to start again, move on with your lives. You won't be alone there. You'll have us and the Red Cross and the British Council for Aid to Refugees, who will help you find your feet and support you." Anh gave the tiniest nod of agreement. Her head was lowered, and Thanh noticed she was biting her lip. He hadn't seen her cry since the day they had buried their parents, and he didn't want to witness it again. He wanted Anh to confirm that everything was going to be alright, that they would find a way to be alright together, whether in the UK or in the US or on Mars. Anh muttered her thanks and got up to leave, and he and Minh followed her out into the dawn breaking over the camp.

He knew leaving Kai Tak had always been the goal, its very purpose, in fact. In front of his brother and sister he put on a brave face, and he could tell they were doing the same. But he wondered if, secretly, they held the same qualms he did, if part of them also wished to stay, where they had school with Mrs. Jones, and Anh worked at the factory, where they could play soccer with the other children and buy Vietnamese food from the hawker near their hut. He thought of his parents and younger siblings sleeping deeply in the nearby earth, of the ocean that would be put between them when they left. As he sat there on the dusty ground, hearing Minh and Anh shuffling their T-shirts and socks into their suitcase, he reasoned that leaving also meant leaving them behind, and that leaving them behind would ultimately lead to forgetting them.

It had been six months since he had last seen his family, and he already had trouble picturing their faces. At night he would lie awake trying to visualize them. He would listen for the pitch of their voices and attempt to recall the way their bodies moved around their house. Sometimes, he would even dream about them, simple scenes that were beginning to merge with his memories and blur into a mirage so that he couldn't always tell if an event had really happened or not. Playing with Dao by the river. Feeding the chickens with Mai and Van. Helping his mother put the baby to sleep. Reading a story with his father. Each time, these dreams would end suddenly, just as he jerked awake, feeling both whole and distressed, crammed between the warm bodies of Minh and Anh. He would replay the hazy scenes in his head, filling in the gaps with his imagination, and then he would try to fall back asleep and reanimate the dreams, but always he would fail.

The door of the hut opened, and one of their dormmates came to sit next to him. Thanh recognized him as one of the men who had seen him tear apart his family photograph earlier that evening, and his cheeks flushed out of embarrassment.

"You're leaving tomorrow, right?" the roommate asked him. He was carrying a guitar, a gift he said he had received from one of his relatives in America the month before and that had created a great stir in their district. On Saturday evenings he played music from his repertoire, everything from lullabies and "Tóc mai sợi vắn sợi dài" to "Aline" to "Love Me Tender." People spilled out of their huts to watch him play or simply left their doors open so his melodies could drift in. It was a thrill to hear those songs out in the open, songs that had been shunned in the years during the war and its aftermath, when singing Western songs was defiance. They were sung in barely audible hums in the privacy of one's own home, just as his mother had done with her yé-yé songs, inseparable from her cooking.

Thanh nodded in response.

"Where to?"

"England," Thanh offered, looking at his feet.

"Oh! Lucky you." He started strumming a few notes on his instrument, the combination of which Thanh had never heard before.

The man began to sing a song, lyrics Thanh could only partially understand, something about the sun coming. "The Beatles. Do you know them?"

Thanh had heard of the band, but he had thought they were American because he thought all the best music came from America. He didn't know this song, and immediately the melody attracted him, a simple tune filled with the promise of better days. His neighbor only knew the first few lines, and soon he moved on to "Yesterday" and "Hey Jude," and when he'd run out of Beatles songs, he went inside their hut, telling Thanh to wait. After a few minutes, he came back out with a piece of paper on which he had scribbled English words, some of which Thanh didn't know the meaning of: "Pink Floyd" and "Led Zeppelin" and "Fleetwood Mac."

"When you get to England, you need to find records by these people," the man said.

Anh called Thanh to come inside, so he hurriedly said his thanks. Delicately, he folded the piece of paper into his pocket, and throughout the rest of the day and during the plane ride, he would pat it repeatedly to make sure it was still there. He wasn't going to live the American dream his father had wanted for them, but he would be in the land of the Beatles and the Stones, of Bowie and Queen. Later, as he worked through the man's list during his first years in the country, their music created a refuge for him. He listened to them and caught a glimpse of an England not quite within his reach, a place beyond the confines of the camp in Sopley and his young age—an England that one day would come to make up his entire world.

*

I realize that there's a lot more I could say.

I could tell people about the rapes and murders, the whispers of cannibalism.

I have read testimonies and books and papers and encyclopedias, and these accumulated learnings have become my burden. But how much should I include?

Sometimes, I get tempted to go the other way, too; to correct the past by rewriting it. Perhaps I could write something like this:

They arrived in Hong Kong, and their parents and younger siblings arrived a few weeks later, baby Hoang waking up from a long nap in his mother's arms. Dao and his brothers played a soccer game

with the other children in the camp, their mothers
looking on from a bench. Mai and Van, inseparable
as always, whispered and giggled to each other about
their classmates and Mrs. Jones. And after a brief
stint at the camp, they all flew to America, where
they were welcomed with open arms.

Yes, that would be tempting, to give them a happy ending.

Or perhaps I could go further. I could add twists and
turns to build in tension. I could write an emotional roller
coaster. I could explore the boat more, for example. Yes,
perhaps I should.

Or perhaps I could point fingers. I could blame politics. I
could blame war and poverty and pirates and the sea and
the storm.

But the more I go on, the more I realize that nothing is to
blame and everything is to blame, intertwined in a medley
of cause and effect, history, and nature.

I am trying to carve out a story between the macabre and
the fairy tale, so that a glimmer of truth can appear.

10

November 1978—The Sea

The sun scorched their faces. The rambutans Anh had eaten a few hours before in Hainan were turning sour in her stomach, the heat and the cradling waves making her nauseous and frail. Her brothers were resting their heads on each of her shoulders. She looked at the little boy sleeping on his mother's lap in front of her, with curly blond hair and blue irises, so different looking than the rest of them and his mother, hints of resemblance visible only in his tanned skin and the shape of his eyes. A noise from the sea grasped her attention, and as she looked out, she noticed a boat coming toward them. At first, she didn't think much of it, and even if she had thought something was amiss, shyness and fear would have prevented her from alerting anyone else. But as the vessel moved closer and her suspicion heightened, she heard fellow passengers becoming agitated, exchanging hasty whispers and confused looks. "Maybe they're just fishermen, or refugees like us," someone said. "Keep calm!" the boatmaster kept instructing them, his voice trembling. He tried to divert their course, but the boat was much slower than the one approaching, weighed down by the crowd of people on board. A smell of urine reached Anh's nostrils. Thanh and Minh woke up and asked her what was happening. Instinctively she said, "Don't worry, it's nothing. Go back to sleep."

The boat was now only a few yards away, and she saw it was carrying three men. They were young, probably not much older than her, and seemed as frightened of the passengers as they were of them. Even the man who appeared to be their leader and was steering the boat had a hint of turmoil beneath his severe guise, looking back at his two companions as if for reassurance, his brows furrowed. But Anh knew that fear was no barrier for viciousness, that it could be its vessel. She caught sight of their knives and the tough expressions they put on as they edged closer, until they were near enough to jump aboard. Her own fear engulfed her until her mind went blank. She embraced her brothers, her hands pushing their faces into her chest. A jolt of prayer vibrated through the people on the boat, washing with the sounds of the unsettled sea. A mother had produced a paring knife and was hastily cutting her daughter's hair, telling her to be quiet. Anh saw fathers and sons crying, grandmothers sheltering the eyes of their grandchildren. She looked death in its face as the leader climbed up in his boat, his sharp knife pointing at the passengers, his white shirt ripped at the sleeves, trousers drenched. Just as he was about to jump aboard, something near the boatmaster caught his eye. His face shifted slowly from ferocious to fearful and then to what looked like shame. For a few seconds, seconds that seemed to encompass all of time, he stayed still, his knife held out in front of him. Finally, he turned his eyes to the hull of the boat and muttered incomprehensible words to his puzzled companions. Without another glance at their would-be victims, the men backed away and settled down again in their boat, sailing away.

The passengers remained silent as it dawned on them that they were still alive and unharmed. The boatmaster bent down to the spot where the man had been staring, smiled, and retrieved a framed photo of Gautama Buddha. He laughed, a laugh mixed with tears that spread through the whole boat, a laugh of relief and disbelief. The sound of prayer resumed, prayers of thanks, jubilant odes to life. "See, I told you it was nothing," Anh said to her brothers. But she refused to let go of them until they had reached Hong Kong and finally stepped ashore.

11

Dao

And I heard Mr. Barnett say "United Kingdom."

I had not heard of this kingdom before.

I wondered if it held knights and princes

or emperors, palaces, and castles.

If it held paddy fields, too, like the ones on the hills near Vung Tham

on which the sun rises every morning.

I wondered what united the kingdom.

If it was held together by a rope or a chain

or if it was a kingdom in which its people were united.

That had not known the division of war.

I went up,

        up,

            and higher still.

I went so high it became dark.

        There was nothing but silence around me
And stars.

    I went up

So that I could see the Earth in its entirety.

        A layer of clouds was slowly making
           its way round the planet.

But I could still make out
its waters and its lands.

        I went up so that I could see

This kingdom that would be theirs.

PART II

12

Operation Wandering Soul: Part I—1967, Vietnam

Within a jungle whose name they don't know, Private Jackson and Private First Class Miller are slowly advancing, pushing aside branches with the tips of their rifles. Their faces are covered in acne, brought about by the heat on their still-adolescent skin. Miller's holding the trigger, ready to pull at the slightest unusual sound, a whisper of breath or the tread of a boot that is not theirs. They're hunched on edge, eyes darting, stomachs rumbling, and backs sweating.

"Are you okay?" Jackson mouths.

Miller nods, although he's aware his heavy breathing and dripping forehead are giving him away. He's carrying a portable PA speaker with both arms, weighing what he imagines a baby elephant must weigh.

They both think this is idiotic.

Lieutenant Smith had come to see them that morning at breakfast—chopped ham, eggs, and powdered milk. "Boy, do I have a mission for you," he told them, smirking, which was never a good sign with Lieutenant Smith.

He presented the speaker to them, pointing to the nearby jungle. "You need to go in there, drop it, not too far from camp, and press play." He took a cassette tape from his pocket with a label on its spine that read, "Ghost Tape n.10." Smith inserted the tape into the player and looked at the two privates, laughing at their bafflement.

"Operation Wandering Soul," he said. "To scare the living shit out of those gooks." The thought, they could tell, delighted him.

Miller and Jackson knew not to ask any questions, and obeyed the order.

Finally, they find an area flat enough to position the speaker without risking it falling over. "Ready?" asks Private Miller, his voice quavering. Private Jackson covers his ears with his hands.

Private Miller presses play, and as soon as he does he winces, having no clue what to expect. Strange, eerie sounds, screams, and wailing emanate from the speaker, chilling them to their core. The soldier's Vietnamese is rudimentary, but in between the shrieks, they untangle a few words: "dead . . . hell . . . home . . ."

The reaction is immediate. The sound of gunfire rises from the jungle like a symphony. The two look at each other, frightened, and run as fast as they ever have back to their base. The distant shouts of Vietcong soldiers mingle with the voices emanating from the tape, so much so that they cannot tell anymore which are real and which are not.

Lieutenant Smith is standing in front of the tent, and when he sees them sprinting toward him he cackles, a laugh that is cruel and crude. He gives them an inquiring thumbs-up, and the soldiers return the gesture, puffing and afraid. "Well done," Lieutenant Smith says. "Now go and clean yourselves up. You both look like shit."

Miller and Jackson grab a bucket of water and try their best to scrub the mud off their boots, firing guns still ringing in their ears.

13

May 1979—Sopley Refugee Camp, Hampshire

Anh and Thanh vomited on the plane. Minh managed to restrain himself until the ten-minute drive to Sopley, when the sausages and eggs he was given on the flight splattered onto his siblings and the car seats. Sophie, the fieldworker who had picked them up from the airport, tried to reassure him. "It's no bother, honestly. You should have seen the family that came last week." They didn't understand everything she said, even though she was speaking slowly, but thankfully she had an interpreter with her, a man called Duong, whose Vietnamese contained dribs of English inflections. Both had welcomed Anh and her brothers with blankets to wrap themselves in but they were still cold, not yet used to the brittle English weather. As Sophie drove, Anh looked out of the window and saw green fields passing by, sheep and horses standing still in the grass, foreign landscapes that were now hers. Underneath the vomit and engine oil, she could smell the fertilizer on the fields, and a warmth began to stir in her at the sign of these new places and beginnings.

When they arrived at the camp, they passed through a military checkpoint that reminded the siblings of war. They remembered soldiers from both sides marching through their village unannounced to set up checkpoints, their intentions always unknown, tension rising in every household. Sopley itself was brutal and sinister, square barracks made of gray concrete laid out one after the other. Sophie and Duong explained that it had been a Royal Air Force base during World War II and that the government had requisitioned the site for refugees just the year before. They showed them to their new residence, hut number 23, which looked strikingly familiar with its three-tiered bunk beds and wrinkled white walls. Anh felt like they were back to square one. "I'm in charge of huts twenty to twenty-five," Sophie said. "If you ever have any problems, please come to me."

The hut had been furnished with a small table and four wooden chairs, a sink, and some plates, glasses, and cutlery. Across the slender tarmac road was a communal kitchen that they could use. "You can decorate the hut as much as you like. I can give you paper and pencils, and you can hang some drawings," Sophie said, looking around the blank room. That night, they had the room to themselves, but another plane, carrying their new dormmates, was due to arrive tomorrow.

"You'll be twelve in total," Sophie said. "It'll mostly

be grown-ups, but there'll be a boy around your age." She pointed at Thanh. "His name is Duc. He's coming with his grandmother."

"Where are they from?" asked Thanh. Anh sensed the nervousness beneath his casual tone, as he tried to find out if this boy would be a friend or a foe.

"From South Central Vietnam, like you," Sophie said. "Duc is just a year older than you."

Thanh relaxed a little. "Oh good," he said. "Maybe we have friends in common."

"Maybe," Sophie said with a mixture of amusement and pity. "Maybe you do, yes."

It was the first time they had had a night to themselves since leaving Vung Tham, the first night that they would not be subjected to a stranger's snores or night terrors. Jet-lagged and dreading the silence, they stayed up late, wide awake and on edge, unsure what to do with themselves. Anh went to the kitchen and cooked the baked beans that Sophie had provided. She stir-fried them like she would have done rice noodles, adding a bit of oil to the pan and burning them slightly. She crossed the moonlit road in her flip-flops, hurrying as the unfamiliar noises of the night, crickets and strange birds and chatter from the nearby huts, reached her ears. The burnt smell followed her inside as she brought the blackened pan back to their hut and began serving the contents on small plates. They also had white bread, but she didn't think to toast it, so it was soggy and soft in their mouths. The whole meal tasted bland and overly sweet, with bitter bits of char in each bite. Anh saw her brothers' thin grimaces as they tried to chew and swallow the food, slowly, with extravagant gulps and munches.

"It tastes . . . different," said Minh, taking a cautious bite of his bread.

She thought that this poor excuse for a dinner marked a failure on her part, a failure at British cooking, her first test of assimilation.

They were orphans now. She hadn't known what that English word meant until a few weeks ago. Now, it branded them, noted in the identification files she had seen Sophie carry and whispered between the adults who cared for them. She recalled her mother's parting words, "Take care of your brothers," and now she was at a loss as to how to behave, stuck between the role of big sister and stern but caring mother. Above all, Anh still felt like a child herself. In private moments, when her brothers weren't inundating her with questions, the colossal role that she held overwhelmed her. It was as if she was drowning, lost in an ocean of unknowns. She longed for guidance, she longed to escape and start a new life, away from her brothers, away from her past, and away from responsibilities and restraints.

Anh asked her brothers if they had enough to eat before she finished her own plate, and then she watched them, goodness and innocence oozing out of them as they brought spoonfuls of overcooked beans to their mouths. She realized that she would never stop trying to protect them.

Just past midnight, Anh instructed Thanh and Minh to get ready for bed, and they obeyed without objection, their eyelids beginning to flutter. Together they hovered over the tiny corner sink, its porcelain cracked and its drain slightly clogged. They brushed their teeth and washed themselves, splashing the cold water onto their faces. When they were done, they got into the pajamas that were folded in the box of donations Sophie had given them—pants and T-shirts embroidered with cartoon characters they didn't know, a brown dog and a pink leopard—and slid under their covers. They had enough beds for each of them, but Thanh and Minh nestled together while Anh took the bunk above, climbing the ladder and slipping into it after she had turned off the light. Throughout the night, the sound of Thanh's and Minh's shallow breathing made its way to her, a hint of life and of their peace.

14

Dao

I have lost my notion of time and space. At first, I struggled. I had not yet learned how to control my new body, or my lack of it. I would jump a little too high, and I would find myself in a completely different place. I would sneeze, and it would be night.

But I have the hang of it now, I think. Ma told me that I need to focus my thoughts on a place and a time, that intent is more important than action.

It was fun at first. One minute I am in a void with other ghosts, and then I focus on Vung Tham and I am there, and then as soon as I feel like it, I can be in England with my big siblings.

There are a million things I would like to ask them. I would like to know what the sausage on the plane tasted like. I would like to know if they feel it when I flow near them. I would like to know if they remember that time I caught a fish in the river that was bigger than my hand and how come they don't cry for us more often.

I thought ghosts could read minds, but there are so many thoughts in each mind, everything is messy and muddled. It's like watching TV with a bad signal, snowy screens, and fizzing voices, a fractured film.

When they laugh, it's like a dagger in my heart, forging the distance between us more deeply. I went back and told Ma this, and she got angry, said, "Don't you want your brothers and sister to be happy?" I was ashamed of my jealousy and selfishness. Mai and Van were snickering at my being told off, so I rose and went back to my room in Vung Tham. But I couldn't sit on my futon. I couldn't sit in the corner of my room and hold my knees to my chest like I used to.

Yes, at first it was fun. But soon, I realized that it is lonely and tiring to be a ghost.

I am invisible and voiceless, floating around until a snippet of conversation catches my ear, and like a spy I go and listen in secret. I cannot stay still and I cannot rest. I cannot sit or lie down.

"It's like looking at the window display of a cake

shop," Mai said. "But we can never go in. And we can't leave either. Just stare or close our eyes."

I am awake and aware,

always on the move,

drifting and roaming

with no end in sight.

15

December 1979—Sopley Refugee Camp,
Hampshire

"We learned about the First World War today," said Minh, fiddling with his backpack straps while they walked. "Did you know that more than a hundred thousand Vietnamese soldiers fought with the French?"

"Of course, I did," Anh said, keen to show she still held more knowledge than her little brothers. "Ông nội spent a year in the South fighting during the war; do you remember? He kept telling us about it before he died, but his stories didn't make any sense. I think he was delirious by then."

"Well, we did multiplications," interrupted Thanh, pointing at himself and Duc. "I had to recite the nine times table, and Mrs. Howard gave me this." He opened his notebook, a gold star sticker shining on the page, and he stared smugly at it.

"It's true," Duc said. "She said she'd never seen some-one recite so fast."

The two boys were in year 5/6 together, and Minh was

in year 9/10, the years being coupled together due to a lack
of funds. Anh was in the adult class in the adjacent Upper
School. They only had lessons in the morning, and their
afternoons were often spent in boredom, waiting for the
day to be over. The camp made attempts at organizing
activities, sewing or technology training or movie nights,
but these were not enough to fill the gaps their days
held, gaps that stood between the refugees and their new
lives, now within reach.

The camp had no cafeteria, no restaurant. Instead
of the bowls of congee that they were so used to being
served at Kai Tak, Ba—Duc's grandmother—would make
them scrambled eggs for breakfast, a slice of spam on the
side. The other residents of the hut were all single adults
or couples, and they mostly kept to themselves, eager to
make Sopley a stopover rather than a home. But Anh and
her brothers formed a kinship with Duc and Ba, becoming one another's anchors in a place where people were
always coming and going. Ba gave them the motherly care
they so longed for. She cooked for Anh and her brothers like they were her own blood, and in exchange Anh
took on the more laborious chores, sweeping the floor and
carrying the groceries. As Ba cleaned up breakfast, the
four of them would walk side by side to the other end of
the camp, to the squat, gray prefabricated buildings that
formed their schools. The windows were covered with
children's drawings and paper garlands hung in the class-
rooms of the Lower School.

On her first day, as Anh had debated what to wear to class, not used to a school without a dress code, she remembered her old uniform from Vung Tham at the bottom of their suitcase. Feeling nostalgic, she unpacked it, the shirt wrinkled, the skirt shorter than she'd remembered. She tried it on but it didn't fit anymore, her shoulders and arms too big, her legs too long and hips too wide. She placed it back into her suitcase and wore high-waisted jeans and a red sweater instead. She was nervous about joining a new school, of the new classmates and teachers she was about to meet, and she tried to imagine how her parents would have reassured her. "What are you so afraid of?" her dad would have said. "They're all in the same shoes as you."

Her mother would have held her and told her she had nothing to worry about, that she was smart and pretty and kind, that everyone would rush to be her friend. So, with her parents' encouragement in mind, she entered and scanned the classroom and sat down next to a girl around her age wearing an oversized denim jacket, whose long, dark, and slightly wavy hair reminded her of her sisters'.

"I'm Bianh," the girl said, making room for her on the desk. "What's your name?"

Although they didn't talk much, over the next few months they became friends, a bond forged by their aversion to verbs and to the letter *r* and Anh's affection for Bianh's doodles, which flowered her notebooks with sketches of their classmates and teachers. The camp had become more cramped since their arrival, an influx of new

Vietnamese people arriving every few weeks. There were now more than a thousand residents at Sopley, all waiting to be given council housing, their refugee status securing them a place in this country, a place they needed more than they wanted.

They ran into Sophie on their walk back to the hut.

"Afternoon!" Sophie called, and Thanh rushed to show her his gold star.

"Well done," Sophie said. "The nine times table is the hardest by far." She gave him a pat on the shoulder before turning to the rest of the children.

"You know, it's going to snow tomorrow," she said, beaming. She knew this was an event they had been waiting for.

They had been at Sopley for eight months, and yet they were still not used to the weather. In September, when the days became shorter and colder and their thin cotton shirts insufficient, they had received a box of warm clothes, donated by parents whose children had outgrown them. It contained hats and gloves, boots and sweaters and warm jackets, which were all too big for Thanh, moving stiffly in them as Anh fought to adjust his coat zipper. She didn't like clothing donations, a reminder of their lack of belonging, their dependence on the kindness of strangers. She had kept the box closed for as long as she could, pushed beneath their bunk beds. Her brothers would curiously lift the lid to peek at its contents, and Anh would frustratedly tell them to keep it shut, while Duc and the other inhabitants paced about the hut in their new sweaters and scarves. But as their shivers grew, she relented, the breezy autumn giving way to an icy winter that turned their breath white when they exhaled. Each morning was colder than the previous one, and their days of humidity and warmth, of flip-flops and shorts and sweat felt so very distant now. But they hadn't yet seen snow, only heard about it through stories, and the phenomenon had taken on a mythical dimension in their heads. When Sophie said that they would finally experience it the next day, the boys let out high-pitched screams of excitement. Once they got home, Duc rushed to talk to Ba, who couldn't speak a word of English, and translated Sophie's words for her.

That night, they went to bed hurriedly, filled with delight at the promise of a snowy morning. Ba hushed them as they leaped around the small, crowded space, the other roommates confused by their sudden excitement, not knowing what the next day had in store. The children let go of the tensions that had accumulated over the past year. They still carried with them their loss, the quarantines and camps and the constant feeling of dread and precarity somewhere in their bodies, but where exactly they didn't know. All they knew was that snow marked something thrilling, a sign that they had made it to a new and strange land, its climate still to be learned.

When they woke at dawn, Minh jumped from his bed and drew the curtains aside to reveal the whiteness. Their roommates groaned, but soon curiosity got the better of them, and they slowly hauled themselves awake. Snow covered the roofs and the cars, the ground and the streetlamps. The residents of hut 23 pulled their coats and boots over their pajamas and stepped outside, not minding the cold, not minding the wind, not minding Ba's meager protests as she stood by the door warily, one foot outside and one still in the warmth of their hut. The intricate, almost invisible flakes melted in their hands and on the tongues the children stuck out to catch them. They were confused by the cause and effect, how such tiny flecks could form a mass that swallowed their boots. It was, for Anh, a given that the snow would fall from the sky in chunks and not in these tiny droplets, like specks of dust. She held out her hand to catch the snowflakes, watching each one melt on her fingers.

At the camp entrance, Sophie was talking to some neighboring villagers and their children, carrying firewood. Anh had seen these people before in passing on occasional, supervised outings. The parents had looked at her and her siblings with pitying smiles, reminding her of the same smile the woman in Hainan had shown them as she handed out rambutans.

Sophie turned and motioned the children forward, suddenly embarrassed when she realized that they were still in their pajamas. "The Evanses have kindly asked if you would like to go sledding with them in the park," she said. "You need to change now; you're leaving in five minutes." She ushered them back to hut 23 before they'd even had time to ask what "sledding" was. Their English had improved greatly over that year, and while they didn't need Duong to translate anymore, there were still some words they had never come across, and "sledding" was one of them.

They climbed the shallow hill in the park, the Evanses and their children leading the way, Sophie and Ba looking up from its base. "Here—Rose and Dan will go first to show you." The Evans children, around Thanh's and Minh's ages, sat on the wooden boards and glided down the hill, their speed increasing as they went. Anh watched, impatient for her turn, imagining the sensation of sailing on a cloud. She was surprised by the assuredness in her movements when she took the sled from Dan and positioned herself on it. For the past year she had been used to asking and not taking. Nothing in her new life was a given. Everything had to be granted to her, by the United Nations or the Red Cross or the Refugee Council. Her heart skipped as she raced smoothly down the hill, her hands gripping the wooden sled and the cold wind smacking her face, her scarf flying behind her.

She ran back up and handed the sled over to Minh with a smile and a nod to assuage his trepidation. "Don't worry," she said. "It's really fun." He took the wooden board, now determined, and with Thanh on his right sledded down and sprinted back up immediately. Anh thought of Mai, Van, and Dao there, too, of discovering this new world with them, a world of white, slippery hills, of icy breath and snowball fights. She imagined them speeding down the hill, their small shrieks of joy echoing throughout their descent. But as soon as it appeared, she brushed the thought away. Today she didn't want to be sad; today she wanted to be a child again. And so, when Minh trudged back up the slope once more, she took the sled from him and said, "My turn."

As midday came, Sophie told them that it was time for lunch. They each said their thanks to the Evanses, the mother giving Anh a hug that didn't feel pitying but warm, Rose and Dan telling her brothers to come visit. They huddled back into Sophie's car, back to Sopley and to hut 23. On the drive they looked into the white gardens of the houses they passed, children in thick coats rolling snowballs around the lawns and piling them on top of one another. When they arrived at the hut, they took off their coats and scarves and boots and went across the path to the kitchen. There, they sat around the dining table in anticipation. Ba boiled a pan of milk and carried it to the table, careful not to spill it, and Anh grabbed the cocoa powder from the top shelf to stir it in. They drank their hot chocolates, like they imagined every other English kid was doing, and discussed their plans to make snowmen and snow angels. They drank and laughed and chatted,

Ba knitting a scarf in the corner while Duc and Thanh planned their afternoon and Minh warmed his hands on top of his steaming mug. Other residents came and went around them as they remained at the table, still and content. And at that very moment, Sopley felt like a sliver of home.

16

July 29, 1979—Downing Street

LETTER FROM PRIME MINISTER MARGARET THATCHER TO THE NGUYEN FAMILY

Dear Family Nguyen,
Thank you for writing to me about the future of the people of your country and your own family. I fully understand your longing to be reunited with your parents.

I know what terrible sufferings have been endured by refugees from your country. That was why I first proposed that the United Nations Secretary General should call a conference to work out practical measures to help them. We are taking a full part in this international effort and have decided to accept another 10,000 refugees into this country.

I know that in the case of your own parents the United Nations High Commissioner for Refugees is making every effort to bring them out of Vietnam and we, for our part, have already authorised their entry to this country.

Like you, I hope it will not be long before you are a united family again.

Yours sincerely,
(SGD) MT

17

January 1980—Sopley Refugee Camp, Hampshire

Anh was chopping vegetables in the kitchen, carrots and snow peas and eggplants. The sticky rice that came with their weekly food distribution was cooking on the stove, and the room was filling with steam, its heat a welcome counter to winter's cold. Ba was stir-frying noodles just a few yards away, the pan making a sizzling sound each time she added drops of oil to the dish.

The week before, Duc and Ba had been called into the Resettlement Office and told that a house in London was available to them and that they would be moving in a week. When they came back into the hut and shared the news with Anh and her brothers, Anh was elated for them, but she was also a little dejected. The closest thing they had to family would soon be departing and leaving them behind.

"We're going to a place called Catford," said Duc. "We'll have our own kitchen and bathroom."

"That's great!" said Minh, and Anh heard the heartache

in his tone. Thanh went to sulk bitterly behind Anh. Part of her wished she could do the same, that she, too, had someone to hide behind.

They prepared a humble feast on the evening of their departure, a tradition in the camp. Huts 20 to 25 were all invited, as were Sophie and Duong and Bianh and Duc's teacher, Mrs. Howard. Thanh and Minh hung a paper garland in the kitchen that spelled "Congratulations," something they had bought with Sophie earlier that day, and Duc carefully arranged paper plates and plastic cups on the table. None of them had hosted anyone since leaving Vietnam. Anh felt at odds hosting in a place that didn't belong to her, a place in which they were guests themselves. She tried to focus on her simmering vegetables and on the evening ahead, keen to give Ba and Duc the best send-off that Sopley had seen.

The guests arrived just as the sun went down, bringing homemade rice wine and crisps and xôi mặn. The kitchen filled up quickly, chatter echoing. The food was set on the table buffet-style, and guests helped themselves, loading their paper plates, which absorbed the dishes' sauces, and complimenting Anh and Ba on their cooking, patting their backs.

"I'm going to go to a real English school," Duc was telling anyone who would listen, his mouth filled with fried noodles. "With English children. I heard they even have a soccer team."

Minh nodded and smiled, looking down at his plate, his

eyebrows slightly frowning. Thanh was still a little woeful, but before the party, Anh had taken him aside and told him to make an effort. "You don't want to end on bad terms with them, do you?" she'd said. "Act like a grown-up, please."

She could tell that he was trying his best, saying "Wow" and "Lucky you" at Duc's stories, his smile overly wide as he gripped his drink. Sophie stood next to Ba trying her best to speak Vietnamese. "We'll miss you," she said. "Me, too," Ba said in return.

Anh spent the whole evening celebrating, asking Duc and Ba questions, making sure everyone had enough food on their plates and drink in their cups, and that Sophie and Mrs. Howard didn't feel like outsiders among the symphony of Vietnamese they had found themselves in. Anh played the perfect host, and yet, deep inside, she couldn't help but sense a shameful hint of jealousy. *Why them and not me?* She so badly wanted her life to begin, too. She wanted her own kitchen and her own bedroom, wanted Thanh and Minh to go to an English school and have English friends. She wanted a place to call home, not a hut in which people were always coming and going. She wanted to settle, not wander.

The last guests left a little past midnight. Anh cleaned the table and scrubbed the pans until the kitchen was immaculate. The next day she and her brothers and Duc and Ba woke up at dawn, careful not to rouse their roommates, all of whom were surely hungover from the night's festivities.

Silently, they left the hut and met Sophie by the entrance to Sopley, shivering and drowsy.

"Ready?" she asked Duc and Ba, putting their luggage in the truck of her car.

They nodded, apprehensive of the unknown that awaited them outside the camp. Ba took hold of Anh's hands, looked her straight in the eyes, and told her, "Cảm ơn cháu." There was not a dry eye on the cold pavement. Thanh, Minh, and Duc embraced like brothers while Sophie watched from the driver's seat of her car, leaving them space for their adieus.

"We'll keep in touch," Anh told Duc, giving him a hug. "As soon as we come to London, we'll let you know."

Finally, Sophie rolled down the window and ushered Ba and Duc into the car. "We want to avoid the traffic," she said, looking at her watch. Around them, the inhabitants of Sopley were starting to rise, lights turning on inside the huts, kitchens filling up. Anh and her two brothers stood by the entry gate and watched the three of them drive off, Duc opening his window to wave at them. They followed the car until Sophie took a left turn, and then Ba and Duc were gone.

18

London, December 30, 2009

DOWNING STREET FILES REVEAL THATCHER'S RELUCTANCE TO WELCOME VIETNAMESE REFUGEES

BY ROB DONNE, CHIEF REPORTER

Downing Street files reveal that in July 1979 Margaret Thatcher's foreign secretary, Lord Carrington, and her home secretary, Willie Whitelaw, ambushed the prime minister into an informal meeting regarding the growing Vietnamese refugee crisis. At the time, refugee camps in Hong Kong held more than 60,000 habitants arriving at a rate of 500 a month, and more than 540,000 refugees had been resettled abroad.

Official minutes from the meeting were released recently under the thirty-year rule, which provides that certain government documents should be released publicly thirty years after their creation. They show the then recently elected prime minister's reluctance to welcome the 10,000 refugees that the United Nations High Commissioner had privately urged her and Britain to take in, and which Carrington told her could be spread over two years. She feared that doing so would result in riots on the streets. As she said, "[It was] quite wrong that immigrants should be given council housing whereas white citizens [are] not."

The minutes also suggest that Thatcher's unwillingness to bring in Vietnamese refugees rested on racial grounds. She admitted that she would rather welcome white refugees "such as Rhodesians, Poles, and Hungarians, since they could more easily be assimilated into British society."

Thatcher suggested to the Australian prime minister, Malcolm Fraser, that the two countries jointly buy an Indonesian or Philippine island, "not only as a staging post but as a place of settlement" for all the refugees. Lee Kuan Yew, Singapore's prime minister, blocked the proposal, fearing the island would become a "rival entrepreneurial city." Australia ended up welcoming 200,000 boat people.

When Whitelaw told her that, according to letters he had received, public opinion favored accepting more of the refugees, she retorted that "all those who wrote letters in this sense should be invited to accept one into their home." She also wondered if the refugees could not simply be "shifted from one warehouse in Hong Kong to another in the UK."

Only a few weeks prior, in June, Thatcher had urged the United Nations to organize a conference to tackle the humanitarian crisis at hand. "I am glad you share my belief that the problem is urgent and that additional measures are desperately needed," Kurt Waldheim, UN secretary-general, wrote to her on June 4. "However, before such a conference is held, I believe careful preparations would be essential to ensure positive results."

On June 8, Lord Carrington wrote to her: "We have so far had an <u>unsatisfactory</u> response to your urgent request to the UN Secretary-General for a special meeting on refugees. Dr Waldheim has passed the matter to the UN High Commissioner for Refugees who is reluctant to call a meeting <u>without firm pledges</u> from participating countries that they would be prepared to take specific numbers of refugees."

As the conference loomed, Thatcher finally relented, conceding that Britain would accept 10,000 refugees over three years, with a preference for those who spoke English.

*

The truth is, I don't want to write about death. I want women to live. I want children playing in fields and piggy-back riding on their fathers. I want family feasts and Sunday outings, school choirs and afternoon naps.

But instead, I rip open wounds I never knew I had. I sit at my computer and dig through remnants of the past: national archives and interviews, newspapers and photographs. I find photos of the war, of children lying dead in front of their burning houses, their ghostly visions following me day and night; of women about to be executed, rebuttoning their blouses.

I am haunted by the three hundred unarmed Southern Vietnamese civilians killed during the Mỹ Lai massacre by US soldiers—their allies. I learn that out of the twenty-six soldiers who were charged for that war crime, only one,

Lieutenant William Calley Jr., was convicted and given a life sentence.

I get angry, sickened into the late hours of the night alone in my apartment. I give up for weeks at a time and watch TV instead.

But I always come back, not because I am drawn to the horrors but because I feel a visceral need to know them. Knowledge allows remembering, and remembering is honoring. I want all the dead to be revered. I want monuments and statues and poems in their honor. I want podcasts and a ten-part docuseries, I want our own *Apocalypse Now.*

In 2009, Lieutenant William Calley Jr. apologized for the first time for his role in the Mỹ Lai massacre. "There is not a day that goes by that I do not feel remorse for what happened that day in Mỹ Lai. I feel remorse for the Vietnamese who were killed, for their families, for the American soldiers involved and their families. I am very sorry."

I want amends and I want reckoning. I want magic powers for the armless and harmless. I want a *John Wick*–style revenge on their executioners.

A few weeks after Lieutenant Calley's sentencing, President Nixon ordered that he be removed from prison and his sentence reduced. He served three and a half years under house arrest and currently lives in Gainesville, Florida.

I want justice and I want peace; I want life and I want delight.

19

February 1980—Sopley Refugee Camp,
Hampshire

"Can I help you?" the salesperson asked Anh. She was
at the gigantic Woolco supermarket just outside Bournemouth. Sophie was doing her own shopping in the endless aisles nearby, putting cornflakes and cans of soup in
her basket. Once a week, they were allowed to go to the
neighboring village's market, where stalls of vegetables
and fruits, meat, and fish were spread out across the main
road. Wary and distant at first, over the course of that
year the grocers had become used to their visits, and some
of them had begun to display prices in Vietnamese and
Cantonese. They were fond of Thanh's cheeky smile and
gappy teeth, Minh's improving English and his resulting
pride. On occasion, the grocers would even slip an extra
apple or a few sweets into their bags. Their youth pro-
tected them from the worst hostilities, but from time to
time Anh would witness older inhabitants of the camp
ignored by local people or nudged aside in lines. "I can't

understand you," the grocers would complain, even if the refugees spoke decent English.

Each time she saw something like this, she looked down, ashamed and powerless, feigning ignorance of what was happening right in front of her. Anh and the other refugees had learned not to handle the fruit and vegetables displayed on the stalls, like she and her mother used to do in Vung Tham, after grocers had complained to the camp about it. If she did, out of habit, the grocers and other customers would look at her as if she were a stray dog. Instead, she had to signal to the grocer how many tomatoes or oranges she wanted so that her own hands, which they imagined were filthy or thieving, were removed from the equation.

It was Sophie who had suggested going to the supermarket instead of the village. Anh was looking for longan, Mai and Van's favorite fruit. They didn't have rambutans or lychees, and she'd given up on finding durian, starfruit, jackfruit, or dragon fruits. For some reason, she still hoped they might have longans, but when she said the word to the man stocking the shelves and explained what it was, he shrugged. "We don't sell those kinds of things here. Why don't you just buy English fruit instead?" She thanked him and picked up some oranges and bananas, trying to seem enthusiastic. She did find a pineapple, which she balked at the cost of but put in her basket anyway, anxious that the thịt kho she intended to make would otherwise be a very meager meal. "All done?" Sophie asked, emerging from the canned goods aisle. Anh didn't want Sophie to see her disappointment, so she said, "Yes, all done, thank you," and on her way to the till grabbed a bouquet of flowers, the cheapest ones on offer, yellow roses with wilting petals.

In the car, Sophie tried to make small talk, to cheer Anh up. It had been a week since Duc and Ba had left, and she tried her best to stifle her lingering jealousy. She'd heard stories of London. That it had a Chinatown where you could eat phở and speak Vietnamese without people chastising you, that it had rows of Chinese and Vietnamese restaurants, that there was council housing filled with people like her. Sophie was watching Anh out of the corner of her eye. "I know it must be a little empty, with Duc and Ba gone," she said. "When you turn eighteen in a few months, you'll be able to get council housing in London, too." But she went on to say that there was no guarantee of when it would be granted, muttering something about Thatcher and housing shortages. "She said she would make home for ten thousand Vietnamese refugees, but where these homes are, it's a mystery." Contempt flourished in her voice. "They're having to place refugees in hotels; can you believe it? She's digging herself deeper into a hole every day, that woman."

Anh remembered listening to the BBC Radio a year before. In clipped English, the broadcaster had read out a letter that Thatcher had written to a Vietnamese boy and his family stuck in Hong Kong, the way she and her brothers had been only months earlier. The three of them were in the kitchen with Duc and Ba and another couple from their hut, all huddled near the radio. They listened attentively as the broadcaster read aloud her sympathetic words, her promise to welcome ten thousand of them. They had cheered at the welcoming and compassionate letter, but six months had now passed, and the camp was becoming overcrowded. Resettlement was scarce, and Anh had wondered if the promise had been an empty one.

For the time being, she and her brothers were stuck in Sopley. It had been more than a year of living in camps instead of a home, and the oppressive atmosphere was starting to take a toll. The previous month, as she was waiting outside the school for her English lesson to start, Bianh had pointed at the barbed wire fence that surrounded the camp. "Do you think it's here to keep us in or to keep people out?" she asked. Anh had only noticed the fence in passing before, first at Kai Tak and now here, not giving much thought to its function. Now, each day, it was all she could see, the metal binding them in as if they were not to be trusted. Any lingering hope that Sopley could be her home dissipated. She sensed a shift in her mood, growing more irritable each day. Minh was a teenager now—fifteen years old—almost the age she had been at the time of their leaving. It was flagrant to her how many more responsibilities she held compared to him, how he got to act as a child while she had had to become an adult overnight. She would snap at him for leaving his dirty clothes on the floor, at Thanh for his habit of chewing with his mouth open. "You're both pigs!" she'd tell them. And she resented her brothers for making her act this way, for turning her into a bad-tempered and weary caretaker, for having stolen part of her youth.

Farmland dashed past the window. As she was getting lost in her thoughts, "London Calling" blared from the car's radio. "See, it's a sign!" Sophie said, turning the volume up. Anh didn't explain that it was unlikely, considering the fact that the song came on a hundred times a day.

Minh and Thanh were finishing up their math class as she got back to the camp. They ran out of the classroom toward their sister to see what she'd bought, and when she showed them the contents of her bags, Minh said, "That's it?" Once more she got angry. For over an hour she'd wandered the aisles looking for shrimp paste and oyster sauce for their parents' and siblings' giỗ—their death anniversary—to no avail. As always, her efforts went unnoticed, her failure instead sticking out like a splinter rubbed at by her brothers.

For the rest of the afternoon, she cooked in silence while her brothers did their homework on the communal table. She missed cooking next to Ba, Duc doing his exercises alongside her brothers, providing her with some respite. Without them, the siblings' relationship was more intense, as if they were constantly stepping on each other's toes. As they grew older, the lack of privacy was becoming more burdensome; they could hide nothing besides their thoughts, and sometimes even those felt like they were on display.

Anh boiled the rice and the eggs and simmered the pork, the noise of her brothers' scribbling pens in the background. The camp had organized a movie night that evening—*The Kid* by Charlie Chaplin—and thus they had the kitchen almost to themselves. Thanh nervously tapped his foot on the floor beneath his chair, which only a year ago he had been too short to do. "Can you stop that noise?" Minh snapped at him. "You're distracting me."

The brothers finally finished their exercises and went to help Anh, setting bowls on the small altar that they had fashioned on one of the kitchen cabinets. They didn't have a family photograph, the sole one that had made the trip with them having been torn up by Thanh back in Kai Tak. Instead, Anh had bought a vase at the Salvation Army shop across from the camp to place at its center. Anh removed the price tag from the flowers, filled the vase with water, and placed the flowers inside, displaying it with incense sticks on either side that Ba had left them. Once they set the caramelized braised pork and the fruit out in front, they lit the incense so that the familiar smell and smoke filled the room, calling their family from Beyond. They knelt in front of the altar and prayed, and only when the incense had fully burned, and their family had had time to eat their meal, did they help themselves to the food. The braised pork was a pale imitation of their mother's, Anh having been unable to find the right ingredients to cook it properly. But Thanh said, "It's very good, almost like Ma's." He and Minh made a great show of asking for seconds, clearly remorseful for their earlier behavior. In turn, Anh was regretful about her own brooding and filled their plates with heaps of meat. She promised them that once they made it to London she would get better at cooking, until they could no longer distinguish between their mother's food and hers.

Always she tried hard to be strong, to be the rock of their family of three, blocking thoughts of her parents and siblings buried in a land that wasn't theirs. Instead, she had focused on school and on raising her brothers, on improving her English and their assimilation. That night, as they lay in bed, she heard a small whimper, followed by sniffling that grew louder. She climbed down the small ladder and found her brothers red-eyed, their noses dripping and their cheeks wet. Her own lips trembled when she saw them in this state. Suddenly, a tide of repressed feelings poured from her like a river overflowing in a storm. They cried together in the same bed, and when they were empty of tears, which turned into a fine crust around their eyes, they told each other stories in hushed tones so as not to wake the others.

They talked about the time Dao caught that huge fish in the river, pride etched on his face as its tail wiggled, his hands barely big enough to hold it still. The time the American soldiers came to their classroom and gave them

chocolate bars, their dark green uniforms the same color
as the trees, the chocolate half melted. They talked about
Vung Tham and their childhood, of their grandmother
smoking opium on their living room couch and her old cat
sitting on her lap inhaling the secondhand smoke. They
talked about the chickens roaming in front of their house,
of the high-pitched voice of the woman who sold tào phớ
near their school.

What they didn't talk about was the constant sound of
aircraft flying over their house, of distant bombs and the
dust that gushed after them. They didn't talk about the
nearby village of Sơn Mỹ burning, of the tales of American
soldiers leaving the place flowing with blood. They didn't
talk of their parents' growing paranoia and fading appearance after the war, of their hushed discussions of reeducation camps and of their neighbors being taken by soldiers
in the middle of the night. By the time she climbed back
into her bed and closed her eyes, a weight had lifted from
her shoulders. It dawned on Anh that they had managed,
for one night, to make the past sound idyllic, a haven of
childhood bliss. Tacitly, they agreed to set aside the relent-
less fear and misery and only focus on the moments of joy
they had shared amid the wretchedness of war. They had
survived the year, the most painful year she could have
ever imagined. And, if they had managed to survive that,
she thought that, maybe, they would manage to survive
whatever the rest of their lives had in store.

20

Dao

I smell the caramelized braised pork

all the way from up here.
And the smell of incense, too.
I follow the dim light of the burnt stick

along with Ma and Dad
and Hoang and Mai and Van.

With the incense lit, everything looks like it's in technicolor, the smoke carving a pathway to their world.

For once I know where I need to go. I am not wandering but on a path.

To a dinner at which I am a guest.

Not just a spy.

"Please help me get a good grade on my math test," prays Thanh. "So I can make Anh happy."

"Please help us have nice lives here," said Minh, which I at first thought was a little too vague for a prayer. But then he added, "And help me make friends like I did in Vung Tham."

It feels odd to have them pray to me—it makes me feel very old and wise.

"Please, help us get council housing in London," Anh says in her prayers. "So we can finally begin the lives you fought so hard for us to have, and so we can make you proud."

I look over at Dad because I'm not sure what to do. Of course, I want to help them get council housing in London. If I could buy them a house I would, but Dad says that all we can do is watch over them, that we must pray for them and love them from Beyond, and eventually their prayers will be answered.

Back in Vung Tham I would pray, too.

I would ask Ông Nội and Bà Nội to help me make friends.

To give me the strength to play with the other children by
the banyan tree.

I would look on as they flicked their marbles across the
ground

as I hid behind Anh,

the small spheres shining as they rolled.

Mai and Van are eating pineapple voraciously,
                        as Ma tells them to slow down,
And I see that the incense

                is almost gone,

         that soon everything will become fuzzy again,

that I will be back to the world of the dead.

I look at them one more time, at the meal that they
prepared for us with such care, the yellow flowers and secondhand green vase,

    and I tell myself that I will do whatever I can

                to help with their prayers.

21

August 1980

Anh couldn't remember ever having a hotter day in England. It was a heat different from the one in Vietnam and Hong Kong, dry rather than humid, a warmth that fell aggressively on her skin. The car was scorching, and Thanh winced as he took his seat while Minh helped Sophie put their bags into the truck. "We can barely breathe," Thanh said as Anh adjusted his seat belt.

Sophie turned to look at them from the driver's seat. "Ready?" she asked, smiling, and they nodded in unison. Thanh waved goodbye to the camp, but Anh wasn't inclined to do the same. Duc and Ba had already gone and so had Bianh earlier this summer, and without them, the place held nothing of significance to her. Their absence had reinstated the camp to what it was, lines of squared huts and barbed wire fences, any traces of its soul vanishing with them.

After a few minutes, Thanh and Minh were sound

asleep, their heads on her shoulders. Anh looked at them one after the other and noticed how much they had grown since Vung Tham. The first, barely visible hints of a mustache were starting to appear on Minh, his jawline squarer, his forehead peppered with acne. Thanh was twelve, his limbs lanky. He was almost as tall as her, but his face was filled with youth and innocence, for which she felt a pang of relief.

They stayed like this for most of the two-hour trip, occasionally waking up at the sound of a loud horn or the jolt of a sharp turn, as the landscapes passed by the car windows, unnoticed.

"We're arriving in London now," Sophie said.

Anh's heart started to quicken, and she took her brothers' hands in hers. They had arrived at their penultimate destination in a journey that had lasted almost two years, a journey that had broken their family and turned their lives upside down with ferocity and abruptness. Now that they were here, Anh was dizzy with excitement and fear but also dragged down by an abiding sadness for having reached the finish line alongside only a third of their team. *Ma and Dad would be proud*, she told herself in a loop. *This is what they wanted for us.*

"A red bus!" Thanh exclaimed, his hand pointing at the car window. They recognized the vehicle from their English schoolbook in Mrs. Howard's class, and in seeing it, they understood that they really were in London.

The busy streets of Wimbledon and Wandsworth and Streatham scrolled by their small windows. There were fish and chip shops and businessmen pushing their way through the crowded sidewalks, bicycles and policemen and tube stations. "It looks *huge*," Minh said, turning to Anh. She could tell that like her he was conflicted, that he, too, wasn't sure how on earth they would manage to walk and live among those hectic streets. In the camps, at least the chaos had been contained: there, they had been with fellow Vietnamese who were living the same plight as them. But here, they would be lost in the wilderness, living alongside English people who had grown up on those streets, who had built and fashioned them; and Anh wasn't sure if they had built them in a way that was meant for her. Finally, Sophie took a left turn and said, "We're here, in Catford."

They stood in front of a long, four-story building, a color between gray and brown. It didn't look like the houses they'd passed in Wimbledon and Streatham, with red bricks and chimneys and pointed roofs, and Anh had to swallow a pinch of disappointment at seeing her new lodging. Sophie stopped in front of a white door, shuffling her bag to find its keys. "There they are," she finally said. They climbed up two flights of stairs and arrived at apartment 3B. They walked through its doorway as silently as possible, as if afraid to make their presence known. Anh heard Thanh's and Minh's loud breathing, their anxiousness feeding the stale air, which had a faint smell of mold. Sophie showed them around the apartment, a short tour, considering its size: one bedroom, a tiny kitchenette, and a bathroom, in which they could hear the sound of a leak dripping. "The bathroom is just for us?" Minh asked, his mouth agape. Instead of a bunk bed, the bedroom had a queen-size double that was big enough for the three of them to share. The sole pieces of furniture in the living room were a brown sofa, a wooden table, and three chairs gifted to them by the Red Cross. "Can we decorate?" Anh asked Sophie.

"Of course," she answered, putting a hand on her shoulder. "It's your home now."

Sophie handed Anh the keys by the entry door. "Good luck," she said. "I'm very proud of you three."

"Can we send you letters?" asked Thanh as he finished hugging her.

"Of course," Sophie said. "We'll keep in touch."

The siblings had experienced many goodbyes in the last two years, but they were still difficult to go through, each parting a sign of their unsettled lives. Yet although Anh was sad and sorry to part ways with Sophie, she was also relieved. She held deep affection toward Sophie and would miss her, but her presence was a reminder of what Anh and her brothers were: foreigners that had to be surveyed and chaperoned at all times. As she hugged her, Anh felt guilt at having those mixed emotions, and she wondered if her heart had hardened over the past two years, if this was the cost of surviving.

The first thing they did when they went back inside the apartment was lie on the bed, their arms and legs outstretched. Thanh and Minh got up and jumped on it as Anh laughed while telling them to make less noise, their hands reaching for the ceiling, something they hadn't been able to do since leaving Vung Tham.

*

The International Classification of Diseases, maintained
by the World Health Organization and used globally as a
standardized diagnostic tool for illnesses, was published in
its eleventh revision (ICD-11) in 2022. This iteration introduced a new disorder called Prolonged Grief Disorder
(PGD). To be diagnosed with PGD, six months must have
elapsed since the death of a loved one and the severity of
grief still high enough to significantly impair one's life, at
work or personally. Some of the symptoms include "confusion about one's role in life or diminished sense of self,"
"difficulty accepting loss," "numbness," and "bitterness or
anger related to loss."

In other words, PGD is diagnosed when one's grief is
no longer considered "normal." There are social expec-
tations that grief will gradually diminish over time, in a
matter of weeks or a few months. Anything besides the

occasional moment of sadness that extends beyond this time frame signals a state of mental illness, which should be treated and resolved.

On the other hand, there are people who do not grieve and who are deemed monstrous. When I was a teenager in high school, I read *The Stranger* by Albert Camus. It was the book all the cool kids were reading at the time, sixteen years old and suddenly cloaked in existential dread, their cigarettes in one hand and the novel in the other as they waited for the school bus. It follows the story of Meursault, a young man living in Algiers who receives a telegram informing him of his mother's passing. He attends her funeral, where he appears dry-eyed, smoking and drinking coffee in front of her coffin. Later in the day, he encounters Marie, a previous acquaintance, and they go swimming and then to the cinema to watch a comedy. When he stands accused of murder later in the book, the prosecutor uses his apparent lack of grief as proof of his soullessness. This, the prosecutor argues at the trial, is a clear indication that Meursault is a murderer: surely, a man who does not mourn his mother must be a monster. He is sentenced to death.

I didn't like the book when I first read it, though of course I pretended I did. I was frustrated by Meursault's passivity, bordering on idiocy, and by the prosecutor's focus on extraneous information. "Overrated," I concluded as I shut the covers and put it back on my shelves.

Four years later, long past high school and secret cigarettes, my great-aunt passed away. She had been ill for
a long time, her memory a shadow of what it once was,
her speech opaque. I didn't know her very well and I was
sad, but our closeness was insufficient to provoke a strong
emotion.

My family and I traveled to America for the funeral,
and I looked out for her oldest son, my great-cousin, at
the ceremony. "He decided not to come," my mother said
when I asked her where he was, and I was stunned. I mentally admonished him. "Shame on him," I thought.

We met my great-cousin the next day outside his
law office for a short lunch. He had steak and wine and
laughed about so-and-so, showing us photos of his recent
trip to Hawaii, no signs of anguish on his face. How cold-
blooded, I thought. Her own son.

The following year, I embarked on a road trip with university friends across America, from the East to the West
Coast. Before our journey began, I paid my great-cousin
a visit. He welcomed me into his house with a warm hug,
offering me coffee and a slice of homemade lemon cake.
As I entered his living room, I saw, placed on an altar on
top of his mantelpiece, a framed photo of his mother, flick-
ering candles and freshly burned incense surrounding it.
Next to it stood a portrait of her husband, my mother's

uncle, who had died about a decade prior, his eyes blinded by the sun, his vintage Ford colliding with a red maple tree. Hanging on the wall was an acrylic portrait that my great-cousin had made of my great-aunt. She had a serene smile on her face, her wrinkles a pale gray and her eyes bright, her nails pristine as always, the way she had looked before the vacancy of her last days. He then led me out of the back door, and I saw roses blooming in his garden, which he had planted on the day of the funeral, while we were at the cemetery. And I felt deep remorse for having admonished him in my youth, for having put him on trial myself.

There is a proper way to grieve in the eyes of others: not too little, not too much. But there is a part of grieving that occurs behind the curtains, a part that is just for us and the deceased. And I suspect it is in this private communion, away from the crowd and the judgment, that we can find solace.

22

1981—London

The unemployment rate was rising and there had been riots in Brixton and Liverpool and Birmingham and elsewhere across the country. They'd caught the Yorkshire Ripper, Diana and Charles were engaged, and John Lennon was dead.

Anh was nineteen now, a real adult, and she had worked hard in the past year to turn apartment 3B into a home. She had made several trips to the local Salvation Army, buying a couple of cushions and a yellowed-white tablecloth, the green vase she had bought at Sopley now their centerpiece.

The apartment gave her a sense of freedom that she had lacked since leaving Vietnam. The barbed wire fence was gone, and she could leave the property whenever she wanted, without alerting any officials to her whereabouts. It made her feel whole again, a citizen whose presence was valid and not surveyed. She was beginning to untie herself from the image of the ragged refugee that she sometimes saw on the covers of newspapers, plastered on the TV; images she would glimpse out of the corner of her eye and turn away from, not wanting to be reminded of what she had been only a year before, a mixture of shame and sorrow growing in her.

She worked at a garment factory, a job that she got through a friend of a friend of Bianh's who heard they were hiring. It was all the way up in Hackney on the other side of the town, and requiring her to rise at dawn, careful not to wake her sleeping brothers, take three different buses, and walk twenty minutes. The pace was even faster than at the factory in Hong Kong, the hours longer, and the warehouse colder. But she enjoyed the repetitive nature of the work, and now that she had the hang of it, she could let her mind drift for hours at a time. She had made friends there, fellow Vietnamese workers who gave her tips on how to fix a clogged sink (pour boiling water into it); how to apply for settlement status (make sure your brothers get a haircut before your appointment); and how to make good canh cải chua (add a bit of sugar to the broth).

There were a few other Vietnamese on the property, but they didn't seem particularly friendly—she had to pass by a group of young men who sat near the entrance to her building, as they smoked and observed her. Duc and Ba lived in a block not far from them, and occasionally she would leave her siblings there in the evening so she could meet up with Bianh and her friends from the warehouse. The first time that she explained the plan to her brothers they were shocked by her betrayal, until their anger mellowed into sorrow and fear. "We haven't spent one night apart since leaving Vung Tham," Minh said, trying to mask his apprehension at being the eldest for the night.

"Stick together no matter what," their father had told them, but he hadn't told them the instruction's expiration date, when they would be allowed to break away from each other. For months, Anh had resisted her friends' pleas, their "You need to have some fun," until finally she caved, guilt ridden and anguished at the idea of abandoning her brothers. She asked Ba if she could drop the boys off for a sleepover, and of course Ba agreed, with her usual peaceful smile, pleased at the prospect of a lively evening to break up her otherwise quiet days. When Anh took her brothers over, she could smell dinner all the way from the bottom of the staircase leading to the apartment, steamed greens and ginger and lemongrass fish. After Duc opened the door, the three boys ran into the living room, Duc showing them his Rubik's Cube with pride, one side complete. "I did it all by myself," he said as Thanh inspected the cube, Minh feigning disinterest at a children's toy. By now, they were used to those occasional nights out and even enjoyed the change of scenery, Ba's superior cooking. "It's not that your food is bad," Thanh told Anh the next morning. "It's just that hers is *really good*."

Anh, Bianh, and their friends would meet up at one

of their houses, taking turns to host, and talk until dawn. They would discuss their jobs, their siblings, and Princess Diana, the boys who worked at the Chinese restaurant near the factory on Kingsland Road, who sometimes asked them out and gave them leftover noodles and rice. The neighbors would bang on the walls and tell them to be quiet, and they would apologize and lower their voices until they scaled back up again. They would paint each other's nails and split a bottle of wine or two or three between them, and the next morning when Anh picked up her brothers, her head would be throbbing, which she made sure to conceal with plenty of coffee.

Chen, one of the boys from the restaurant, asked Anh out for a drink in Islington, right by Highbury Fields. She ordered a gin and tonic, and he paid for it, the first time a man had paid for anything for her. They spent the evening talking about this and that, about his childhood in Croydon and helping at his father's restaurant, about his grandparents immigrating to the UK in the 1960s to become agricultural workers. When he asked her, "What about you, what's your family like?" her heart thumped, and she became quiet. She took a sip of her drink and smiled, saying, "My brothers and I moved here two years ago. We were in Hong Kong for a bit and Vietnam before then." Before he had time to respond, she asked him more questions, about Croydon and restaurants and China, had he ever been and would he ever go.

The next morning, she woke up filled with guilt. She
wondered why she had balked so strongly at the mention
of her family, if it was from shame of her past, or prudish-
ness, or the Pandora's box of emotions she was sure would
open if she started talking about her history. She feared
appearing reluctant, that her dread had come out as aloofness. However, it was also the morning of Minh's birthday,
and she had a cake to prepare, which distracted her from
her scurrying thoughts.

Minh woke up around noon just when Anh was coming
back from the grocery store, his face still half asleep, his
hair untidy and greasy with remnants of the gel he layered
on every morning. His mustache was fully visible if still
sparse, and he was now taller than their father, something
Anh could not get used to, the upward tilt of her head every
time she had to talk to him unnatural. "Happy Birthday,"
she told him, hugging him. He muttered his thanks and
poured cornflakes into his bowl, nonchalant and drowsy,
as Anh began to whisk the sugar and the eggs and the flour
and butter.

"I'm sixteen now," Minh said, chewing his cereal. "Do
you know what that means?"

Anh was whisking away, the batter becoming thicker,
the clumps smoothing.

"No," she said, only half listening. "What does it mean?"

"It means I don't have to go to school anymore," he
answered. "And I've decided I won't be going back."

The whisk fell into the bowl with a thump as it slipped from her hand.

"What?" she said, raising her voice. Thanh came from their bedroom, alarmed by his sister's anger, which rarely emerged.

"I got a C on my O-Levels," Minh continued, calmly. Anh could tell he had rehearsed this conversation in his head, that he had his arguments on the tip of his tongue. "There's no point in me going anymore. Let's face it. I don't have the grades to get a grant. I might as well start making money, like you."

Anh picked up the whisk and started beating the batter with crushing vigor, her hand slightly shaking. At first, she didn't say anything, focusing on her cake, sensing Minh and Thanh's eyes on her.

"It's not what Ma and Dad would have wanted," she said, finally. "You're giving up on yourself." She could hear the curtness in her tone, and it surprised her. Minh's intent wasn't that ludicrous: many of his classmates would do the same, and she dared to entertain a thought at the back of her mind: they could really do with an extra salary. But like her parents before her, she couldn't help but hope that her brothers would go to university and embark on lengthy, illustrious careers in science or finance. She didn't want to imagine what the future held for him now, his mediocre O-Levels his only diploma, his bad English following him everywhere.

"Let's face it. Ma and Dad's plan didn't go as they

wished from the start," Minh said with a shrug. "I'm just being realistic."

Thanh moved around the kitchen helping Anh with the cake, trying to play peacemaker. He looked back and forth between his siblings, worried, silent.

"You're going to regret it," Anh said. "When you see your friends and Thanh go on to do better things than you."

She used her stern voice, the one that had worked so well in Kai Tak but which had lost its impact in the three years since. Instead of listening, Minh just gave an exasperated sigh.

"I don't have any friends," he said, standing up to leave the room as Anh opened the oven door and slipped the cake in. "Plus, you're not Ma. I don't have to listen to you."

Deep down, she understood him. As much as she envied her brothers for having the chance to study, she was also relieved that she didn't have to attend an English school. She imagined the pale girls with their red or blond hair staring at her secondhand uniform, the teachers mispronouncing her name, her accent the laughingstock of the playground. She saw Minh come home day after day sullen and drained before locking himself in his room, and she wondered if she would have been like that, too. One dinner last fall, she noticed a blue and purple bruise blossoming around his eye and a red scratch on his cheek. She asked what had happened, but he said, "It's nothing," and left the table, his bowl of rice still warm. She could feel him slipping away from her, the distance lodging between her questions and his silences, and she was at a loss on how to bridge that gap.

Thanh had integrated better than Minh, Anh knew. His voice was now an octave deeper, as he did his best to juggle that awkward transition between childhood and adolescence. His Vietnamese accent was less prominent, and he had a cheerfulness that made him likable to his classmates, even the toughest ones. He talked about Mikey and Jamie like they were old friends, trying to explain their inside jokes at dinner while waving his chopsticks around. On Saturdays he played soccer with them, the grass pitches much more pleasant than the dusty outlines in Kai Tak. When he'd brought these two friends over for lunch after a practice in May, it was the first time they had ever hosted English people, and even though they were children Anh was nervous. She spent the whole night before cleaning the house, going over the meal she would prepare. As they arrived, their clothes and hair filled with earth and grass, she realized that they would not care about cleanliness.

They ate their bowls of pasta voraciously, not paying Anh much attention, instead talking about soccer and school. And she was grateful because she had no idea what to say to them. Afterward, they went to the bedroom and listened to the Clash and Pink Floyd on tapes that Thanh had begged Anh to buy for him in exchange for good grades or helping around the house. She held on to him as much as she could. He was her last hope of family prestige, of diplomas and business suits. She tried to help him with his homework, but her memory of algebra and geometry were hazy, her English worse than his. Duc was in the class above him, and sometimes she would ask him to come over so he could tutor Thanh. In return she gave him a few pennies she had managed to save by skipping lunch or dinner. At first, he objected to taking her money, but she made it a source of pride not to take charity from a child.

There were lighter moments, too. Moments in which Anh sensed herself merging with the city and its inhabitants. Like the time, after months of pleading, that she relented and took her brothers to the Odeon on Leicester Square to see *Raiders of the Lost Ark*. She found the movie dull and couldn't follow the plot because the characters spoke far too fast, too American. She suspected her brothers didn't exactly know what was happening either, but they were elated, cheering for Harrison Ford, twisting in their red velvet seats, spilling popcorn all over the floor.

The next day, they made the journey to central London, bus 14, then the Jubilee Line, then bus 47, hopping off at Dean Street and zigzagging the streets of Soho to Wardour Street. There, they bought red bean buns from the Chinese bakery and bánh bao from the Vietnamese lady, who greeted them with a huge wave and eager smile, used to their monthly visits.

They went to Loon Moon and bought soy sauce and

fish sauce and oyster sauce, longans and incense. When they were done with their shopping, they carried it all home in heavy bags that would cause stiffness the next day, up the two flights of stairs and into their small kitchen. That night, even Minh's mood was lifted as he helped Anh with dinner. She prepared nước chấm, and he chopped green onions. He paused for a moment and said, "You know, I really don't know what Thanh and I would have done without you." Then, blushing, he went back to his onions. Anh felt the rips he had torn in her in recent months begin to sew themselves back together, like the many pieces of fabric she had stitched together at the factory. She gave Minh a kiss on the back of his head, and when Thanh entered the kitchen, asking, "What's for dinner?" she told him that if he had helped with the cooking, he would know.

23

Dao

Thanh and Minh and Duc were walking back from the park.

They emptied their pockets and counted their coins

and bought an ice cream each

a mint choc for Thanh, a cone for Minh, and an orange pop for Duc.

They were slurping away, and Thanh said the cold hurt his teeth, and Minh's brain froze for a second. I did my best to keep up with them as I heard fragments of Duc and Thanh talking about school, about their grades and girls and soccer and their future.

Minh was walking a little behind them. He was listening, like me.

His head was stooped low, and he looked wistful, I thought.

We walked by the unemployment office and the queue was
spilling out on the sidewalk;
                              it even had women with strollers
                                   and babies in their arms,
                    men in suits and some in T-shirts,
some old and some young.

After a little while I got tired of listening

          and following

                    and looking

                              and so I went back to the void.

"Where were you?" Ma asked, her hands on her hips. "You
need to stop following those poor boys around."

"But Ma, I get bored in here," I said. "Everything is always
the same here. I'm always the same."

And then I went to see my sisters and told them about all
the different kinds of ice cream that fit in a tiny, pink truck.

24

October 1984—London

"Thank you. We'll call you back if we're interested."

The lady shook his hand and guided him out the door. He'd heard the same words yesterday, and the day before, and the one before that, too. He'd seen the "Help Wanted" ad in the grocer's window, written in big, bold letters that stood out from across the street, and he thought he'd give it a go.

Each time it was the same, a ritual of embarrassment that he regretted initiating. He would enter the hardware store, restaurant, supermarket, anywhere vacancies were listed. He would approach an employee, who would bring him to a manager. The manager would glance at him and sometimes sigh, sometimes smile, conducting the interview right there and then, on the spot. They would start by introducing themselves. "Minh," he would say in response, shaking their hand. And they would reply *"Mean?"* and he would say *"Minh,"* the position of the tongue slightly different, only grazing its palate instead of leaning on it. Then the manager would move on swiftly and ask him about his job experience. But there wasn't much to say. For the past three years he'd done only a few menial jobs, scattered across various fields, month to month, without any steadiness to show.

He'd had a grace period after he'd left school, but then his sister had started pressuring him to get a job. "You can't sit around all day while I'm out working my arse off making money for you," she told him. Without too much complaining, he started looking, and in the end, Anh got him a job at the Chinese restaurant near her work. For months he cleaned dishes in the cramped, steamy kitchen, scraping the rice out of the bowls, the glistening meat sauces sticking to his fingers. During his half-hour lunch break, he smoked cigarettes with the waiters in the alleyway at the rear. It was clear they were more interested in his sister than in him, and he used this to his advantage. He would slip hints regarding her personal life, that she came home pretty late last Saturday and that she was on the phone a lot. They would pretend not to care but listen attentively, and he would enjoy the attention, seeing them grasp at his every word. He came home exhausted, smelling of grease and fried oil but fulfilled by his day's work, proud of the money he'd earned. But after less than a year, as unemployment increased and customers decreased and the Falklands War broke out, the restaurant had to make some quick cuts, and he was the first one to be let go.

At his sister's insistence, Minh got in touch with the An Viet Foundation, a newly founded center that was supposed to help Vietnamese people find housing and jobs in London. He and his siblings had attended one of its social events, a barbecue in East London in which they'd mingled with fellow countrymen and women. They were mostly families with young children, the few men his age were still in school or now employed and were unimpressed by his dropping out and being made redundant.

"I can't find anyone I can get along with," he told Anh, a skewer of lemongrass chicken in his hand.

"Just make an effort," she said. "You're the one who keeps saying we need to get out more. Make small talk to people; you never know, they might help you."

They stayed for a couple of hours, until he could tell that even Anh had grown tired of the conversation, of the "How old is your child?" and "We come from Vung Tham, and then we went to Kai Tak and then Sopley," things they were keen not to divulge too much information about.

In the end, the foundation helped him get a job at a nail salon owned by a Vietnamese woman called Loan. She watched his every move with eagle eyes, following him around, pestering him to clean the towels and rearrange the polishes and answer the phone with more enthusiasm, more enthusiasm, always. Yet after eight weeks of toil, he still couldn't master the basic skills required for the job, the subtlety needed to file nails and paint them without spillages, and once again he was let go. After that there was the McDonald's, but his English made him falter, and he could not keep pace. Often, he had to ask customers to repeat their orders, or they asked him to repeat their totals, sometimes cursing at him, "Speak English," at best, "fucking chink" and a gob of spit launched at him at worst. So he was let go there, too, his manager patting his back, saying, "Maybe you can get some English lessons and come back."

It would have been different in America, he thought, making his way home from the grocery store. They had jobs in America, and in America there were more of them, a real community of Vietnamese and Asians instead of just a few clusters scattered across London. He'd heard of cousins of friends opening their own restaurants and making good money, of Chinatowns sprawling across whole neighborhoods, not just over a couple of streets. He'd heard that in America you could be Vietnamese and succeed, that America was built by people like him, refugees and strangers in strange lands.

Minh had vague memories of an uncle there, someone they were supposed to have joined had his father's stupid plan worked. When they were still at Sopley, he'd asked Anh about this uncle, but she briskly changed the subject, claiming she had no idea where he lived or what he did, that she wasn't even sure they knew his full name. He understood that this was a delicate subject for her, that she didn't wish to explain. In truth, he felt the same way. After all, it was his uncle who had planted the doomed idea into his father's mind. He let the matter go, and over the years, the uncle became a pale, distant myth to him, a faint vestige of a life that could have been.

Instead of being in America, he was roaming the streets of London alone, jobless and parentless. For that, he harbored bitterness, at who or what he wasn't sure, but the bitterness was growing each day as he lost the innocence of his youth. He could feel his skin searing and regrowing thicker and stiffer at each "chink" and each "ni hao" and each slitty-eye gesture thrown at him. He was overwhelmed by the bleakness of his life, by the towering odds stacked against him, by prejudice, and by the growing unemployment rate and his wobbly English, and he wondered what the point of it all had been. If his family had stayed in Vietnam, they would still be together now, and maybe they would have managed to make a life for themselves, to move on from the war. They might have even moved to a big city like Hanoi or Saigon. If they had stayed, they would belong, and belonging was all he longed for.

He saw the other three Vietnamese men from the council estate standing near the doorway to his building, leaning on the brick wall, and approached them to say hello. They were older than him by a decade or so, but he liked spending time with them, feeling grown up as they smoked together in front of the low-rise blocks. He would linger as they talked politics, nodding vehemently at their wise words. "That bitch.

How can you expect they'll give jobs to us if they don't even have jobs for themselves? We only get the scraps, I'm telling you." Sentences he would memorize and reuse later when talking to Anh, though she would dismiss him and say, "You should be thankful for what we've got."

The men acknowledged him with a nod. Lang, their unofficial leader, passed him the spliff they were sharing. Minh inhaled and tried to suppress a cough.

"What's with the face?" asked Lang as he took the joint back. Minh told them about the failed job interview, about being let go from jobs he didn't even want in the first place, about the "will call you if we're interesteds" and the silences that followed. They watched him intensely as he spoke, and when he was done, the men threw furtive glances at Lang, as if anticipating his response. Lang was looking down at the spliff between his fingers, deep in thought, and then he asked, "How old are you again? Do you know your way around here? Can you leave your house at night?"

When Minh answered twenty, yes, and yes, Lang stared at the spliff again. He brought it to his lips and took a long drag, the smell and smoke growing thicker around him.

"I might have a job for you," he said, handing it back to Minh.

25

Operation Wandering Soul: Part II—
1984—Boston, USA

With the help of five other honor guards, Sergeant Jackson took hold of the flag draping Sergeant Miller's casket and began carefully folding it, thirteen times, stars pointing upward.

They had both been promoted toward the end of their service, two months before the fall of Saigon. They'd taken the same flight back to the States, and as they were about to go their separate ways, they embraced like brothers. But once you experience the carnage of combat, everything else feels bland, the small talk and bottles at shabby bars too stark a contrast to the thick jungle and the deafening sprays of bullets, comrades bleeding to death in their arms. And so they drifted apart, only meeting up every couple of years for a beer and an evening of reminiscing. The wrinkles slowly replaced their adolescent, acne-covered skins. The last time they'd seen each other they had both noticed their hair had gotten a little thinner and grayer, their bellies and faces a little plumper.

Jackson took great care in folding the flag, smoothing the cotton with the tip of his fingers, the fabric smooth in his hands. Miller had managed to survive a whole war, he thought—the fires and the guns, the bombings and illnesses and countless wounds. And yet he had not managed to survive a moving van, something so banal, going thirty-two miles an hour, not even fast, not even foolish. It knocked him dead just as the sun's early rays began to peek above the horizon, his wife and kid a few yards away inside the house, still sound asleep. Of course, Jackson had heard gossip that undermined the official story. The levels of alcohol and Xanax found in his friend's body, the driver's sobriety and his reputation for cautious driving. He had heard that the neighbors recalled Miller's screams at night, the light in his bedroom turning on and off again until the early mornings, the bottles of whisky overflowing in the garbage can.

Once the flag was reduced to a small triangle of blue and white stars, Jackson presented it to Miller's widow, Martha, who accepted it gratefully. "Thank you," she said. "He always talked very fondly of you, you know. Of your days roaming around in the jungle." She held the hand of her youngest son, who looked at Jackson with deep consideration. Jackson knelt down in front of the child to pat him on the head and shake his hand. Out of the corner of his eye he caught sight of an old man in a wheelchair, and he felt a thump in his chest. He turned his attention to the man, recognition forming on both their faces.

At the reception, Lieutenant Smith told Jackson his legs had been paralyzed not long before the fall of Saigon, when a bullet lodged itself deep in his spine. "The bastard," he said. "Only half an inch to the side and I would still be standing like a young man."

After the banalities of catching up, anecdotes about their wives and children and their lives after the war, they found they did not have much else to say to each other. Their conversation came to a natural end, both men using the silence to down their drinks. Jackson looked at his empty glass, the ice cubes tinkling. There was a question that had been on his mind for the past twenty years, one that he and Miller had often discussed at the bar until late, coming up with various theories, all of which seemed ludicrous in the end. "We should just write to Lieutenant Smith and ask him," Miller had said the last time they saw each other. "What do we have to lose?" He had leaned on his chair, Jackson remembered, grinning. "Another round, my friend!" he had called to the barman.

"Lieutenant Smith," Jackson began. His voice was shaky, as he was reduced to the twenty-one-year-old self he had been back then, terrified of his superior, terrified of doing or saying the wrong thing. "What was Operation Wandering Soul?"

And Lieutenant Smith smirked, the same smirk he had given the boys twenty years prior.

"There's a tradition in Vietnamese culture," he said. "They believe that you need to give your dead a proper burial in their hometown. If not, their souls are cursed to wander the earth aimlessly, as ghosts." He looked down at the bottom of his empty glass, his smile slowly fading from his face, a frown forming in its stead. "Their soldiers were dying. Every day, more dead than they could keep up with. Just like ours. They couldn't afford to observe their burial rites. We thought we could take advantage of that. We wanted to scare those gooks, those Vietcongs, I should say. We thought if we played tapes that sounded like their dead comrades, they might get scared or become demoralized."

Lieutenant Smith let out a long sigh, and Jackson realized that he was an old man now, with an arched back and distant memories, and in that moment he, too, felt the years catching up with him. The arrogance of their youth was gone, their black-and-white vision of the war replaced by a muddle of gray. Jackson stayed quiet, taking this information and vision in, his mind drifting.

"I see," he said. "I had guessed it was something like that. Some sort of psychological tactic."

Jackson looked around the room. There was something about their setting, their comrade's funeral and his wake, that made more blatant the operation's cruelty. As other mourners circulated around Miller's living room, in which he had sat and drank and watched TV only the week before, this fact did not escape either man. The folded flag, the honor guards, and the gun salute. Didn't they believe in burying their dead properly, too? He had been a stranger on their soil, Jackson thought, and he had conducted a blasphemous operation. He had mocked them and their convictions, which were not so distinct from his own.

As he stood there, Miller's portrait propped on an easel in the corner of the room, the sounds of his widow's weeping in the background and his child roaming around, Jackson considered the tape again. The agonized wails of the deceased, far from home, alone and aimlessly roaming the Earth. He thought about Miller's drinking and his night terrors, and he wondered if you could be both alive and a ghost, if you could be both awake and a wandering soul.

"We really did try everything," Lieutenant Smith said. He turned his wheelchair around and went to refill his glass at the bar.

26

February 1985—London

It was close to midnight, and Thanh was sitting next to her, his hands over his head, studying for his A-Levels. Anh brought the blanket from their room and wrapped it around his shoulders. She read the headline of the newspaper that she had picked up outside the train station, MINERS' STRIKE COMES TO AN END.

Outside, snowflakes were visible beneath the streetlamp's glow. She peered over Thanh's textbook, triangles and circles and numbers. He looked up at her with eyes that said, "Stop bothering me," and so she went back to her chair, drinking her mug of steaming tea. He wasn't the best student but not the worst either, getting Bs and Cs and the occasional A, often in math and physics. "Maybe I could work in astronomy," he'd told her the week before. He had looked embarrassed by his ambitions, as if he had uttered a flamboyant and ludicrous fantasy outside of his reach. "It pays well," he said with a shrug, "but it's very competitive." She was in awe of his willpower, proud that he hadn't given up like his brother.

She heard the scribble of his pen and his tapping foot, and she wished she could help him achieve his dreams. But she knew she didn't have the knowledge to do so, and her secret, wild hope that her brothers would become world-renowned scientists or businessmen had begun to fade. More than for the money or prestige, she thought their success might make her own sacrifices worthwhile, that it would give deeper meaning to the labor she'd done to provide for them over the years, her aching back and pricked fingers all small hindrances for a much bigger goal. If the three of them did not achieve success here, their family's demise had no meaning, no overarching resolution.

Minh was out with friends, and Anh was half staying awake to await his return but also partly because she simply couldn't sleep. She had become a nocturnal animal in the past few years and found comfort in the stillness of the dark. She was now smaller than both her brothers and wearing one of Minh's hand-me-down sweaters, holes under the armpits and on the elbows. She was starting to feel more and more useless, a burden even, outgrown, both mentally and physically. She looked out the window, and the snowflakes reminded her of sledding in Sopley, Minh's apprehension and Thanh's resonant jolts of joy, the Evanses' and Sophie's kind encouragements. They hadn't been sledding since then. Every year the snow made its way back to them, and every year their delight at it diminished, its coldness more taxing than heartening.

Anh didn't know Minh's friends or what they did for a living, and he refused to tell her. But she knew the smell that covered him when he got back late at night; she wasn't a fool. During the day, he worked part-time at the Tesco down the street and made enough money not to ask Anh for much. He slept on their living room sofa, their bed too small for three adult bodies, their need for privacy growing. She wasn't his mother, and there wasn't much she could do; she couldn't pester him the way their ma could have. She didn't have the authority, and she didn't want to replace her, didn't want to feel like a fraud. Instead, she mostly stayed quiet, besides a few remarks or questions. She tried to convince herself that her brothers' lives weren't hers to control, that they were now adults, no longer her burden, and that she had to let them go.

Thanh was beginning to yawn, and she was pulled from her thoughts by the click of the lock turning and the door opening. Minh came in, his eyes red and vacant. Maybe it was her sprawling thoughts or the brisk cold, or seeing Thanh study so hard, or the fact that she was hungry, but that night, she did not want to stay quiet.

"Where have you been?" she asked. Minh didn't answer, going silently to open the fridge, glancing up and down at its shelves.

"There's no milk," he said.

"I told you to buy some this morning. Seriously. That's

the only thing I've asked you to do all week. You *work* at a grocery store."

He muttered an apology and poured himself a glass of water. He stood by the sink drinking as his siblings observed him, Anh fuming and Thanh on edge. He put his glass in the sink and grabbed a banana from the bowl next to it. Anh told Thanh to go to bed, and after feeble protests, he got up to leave, taking his pens and books with him. She let Minh take a bite of his fruit as she gathered her racing thoughts.

"You can't be out late at night like this," she announced. "It's dangerous. And you can't be doing drugs, Minh. We're not even citizens yet. Do you know what would happen if you got caught? They could kick us out!"

He chewed his banana for a long time, his back resting against the fridge, slouching. A car honked outside their window, disturbing the night, its coldness creeping through the thin walls of their apartment.

"You're selfish. Do you even know what would happen if we went back to Vietnam?" she asked. "We have *nothing* there. Do you want that for Thanh? For you?"

His continued nonchalance only made her more irritated. She wanted to shock some sense into him, wanted to provoke a reaction. But he just stood there and looked at her, his thoughts illegible, and once he had finished eating, he said calmly: "Instead of worrying so much about me and Thanh, maybe you should start worrying about yourself."

She hadn't expected those words, and she didn't know

what he meant by them. She didn't need to worry about herself. She had a job and friends and sometimes even went on dates; she was living a perfectly fine life. Yet she couldn't deny that there was a tiny voice at the back of her head that had fashioned itself upon arriving in London, a voice that stirred when she heard Minh's words, which told her that she wasn't doing enough, that she wasn't enough.

"Do you want to work at that factory all your life?" he continued. "Do you really think that's what Ma and Dad wanted for you?"

"You didn't mind me working there when it paid for your meals and clothes," she said, stung by his vicious tone.

"You keep telling Thanh and me to work harder, but look at you," he said, ignoring her retort. "You haven't even tried to do anything with your life. You're still doing the exact same fucking thing you were doing back in Hong Kong."

His words pierced her more deeply than anything he had said before. She knew that they were true, that he was voicing what she had tried to hide from herself for a long time. She wasn't fulfilled or happy working at the factory, and she could do more with her life; the factory was her choice and not her fate. Even Bianh had started her own clothing business, and she had employees of her own now, a small workshop in Dalston that made T-shirts for children. Anh knew that the Refugee Council could help her get another job or even to go back to studying. Sophie had told her that many times in Sopley. But at the factory she was safe; she could speak Vietnamese and hide beneath its high, dirty roof; she could pretend that she was back in Vietnam for a few hours. She didn't want to apply for a job in the real world; she didn't want to study for tests and face failure. She didn't want to experience rejection—she had already been rejected from her own country and from America. All she wanted was acceptance, and the factory accepted her.

"You're as much of a failure as me."

At that last strike, her initial shock waned, and she got angry, furious that he dared to say that to her. For seven years she'd dragged him and Thanh everywhere, cared for them, fed them, and washed them. She'd had to dry their tears and encourage them at school, to push them to make friends and to assimilate. She'd had to put her needs last, to be their role model and guardian, and he was throwing it all back in her face like dirt. Her mug shook in her hands, her body tense and her spirit spiteful.

"I've given everything to you. I didn't ask for this. I could have done so much more without you holding me back. You've ruined seven years of my life."

Anh regretted the words as soon as they left her mouth, and she felt tears forming. Behind his vacant eyes she could tell her words hurt him, his half-eaten banana folded in his hand. She grabbed her mug of tea and stood up abruptly. The chair's creaking resonated into the room's silence, and the newspaper fell to the ground. She brushed past her brother without looking at him on her way to her bedroom, shutting the door behind her.

*

In her essay "Emotions as Judgments of Value," the American philosopher Martha Nussbaum explains that the process of grieving differs from culture to culture. You have the Ifaluk, residents of the Caroline Islands, who believe that those who do not cry loudly at a death will become sick later on. Ifaluk wakes are filled with crying, "from low moaning to loud, wrenching and mucus-filled screaming to wailingly sung poem-laments." At the other end of the spectrum, you have cultures like the Balinese, who believe sadness is detrimental to one's health. Instead of wallowing in despair, they prefer to move on swiftly from a beloved's passing by acting cheerfully and distracting themselves with traveling and outings.

In Anglo-Saxon, stiff-upper-lip, Christian-influenced cultures, the news of someone's passing is often met by those unaffected by it with appeasing, veiled assurances. "He's in a better place" and "She gets to be with [other deceased loved one] now" and "Death is just the beginning." Sentences hinting at a Beyond, still shrouded in alluring mystery. "Although people who have a confident belief in an afterlife still grieve for the deaths of loved ones, they usually grieve differently, and their grief is linked to hope," Nussbaum says.

In the South Sulawesi region of Indonesia, the Torajan people retain the bodies of their deceased loved ones so that they can live at home with them, sometimes for decades after their passing. The chemical formalin is injected into their skin to preserve them, leaving a strong smell in the house. The corpses are bathed and groomed, given food and cigarettes, and the children play and chat with them throughout the day. Finally, months or sometimes even years later, once the families have saved up enough money, a lavish funeral takes place. Relatives travel from all around the world for the occasion, buffaloes and pigs are sacrificed, and the bodies are placed in family tombs with money and goods, necessities for the afterlife they are about to join. Every few years the bodies are taken out to be groomed again and photographed, fed and cleaned, until the celebration is over, and they return to their resting place.

For my whole childhood, I had only attended the funerals of Vietnamese relatives. Officially, Vietnam is an atheist country, as is common in Communist states. Perhaps as a result, the ceremonies are not extravagant affairs. The

funerals take place in cemeteries, often led by a priest.
There are no long, solemn speeches, no procession or pall-
bearers. Mourners dress in black or dark gray, but there
are no other restrictions as to what people wear, most preferring comfort to refinement. I remember, at Ba's funeral,
I went to say goodbye at the open casket. My mother was
holding my hand, crying, as her brothers rested theirs on
her shoulders. Other guests took photographs of Ba's
resting face, of her casket and beautiful white dress. Her
grandson Duc placed a small knife on her stomach, gently. "To protect the soul from bad spirits," Dad whispered
in my ear, intuiting my question. Duc kissed his grandmother's forehead goodnight, and we began making our
way to the cemetery. As Ba was lowered to the ground,
iPhones and Androids snapping photos, I spotted a guest
(I am not sure who) wearing a black hoodie adorned with
Jack Skellington's face from *The Nightmare Before Christmas*, the Pumpkin King of Halloween Town—the large,
goofy skull and deathly symbol proudly on view across
the cemetery.

The first Christian funeral I attended, at twenty-one, was
for my best friend's mother. I wore a black turtleneck and
dark gray jeans, my hair in a messy bun. I didn't own any
smart black shoes, so I wore my black sneakers instead,
thinking they would be fine and color appropriate. When
I arrived at the church, I saw all the women in tight black
dresses, pearls on their necks and ears, sleek pumps on

their feet. The men wore black or gray suits and cuff links, a black Cadillac was parked out front, and beautiful flowers lined the church. As I took in the scene and the guests gave me puzzled looks, a great wave of embarrassment hit me. I was clearly underdressed, which, at a funeral of this kind, displayed a lack of respect: I was no better than the Jack Skellington–wearing guest who had struck me years before.

Afterward, at the reception, I apologized to my friend, admitting to her my mortification.

"I had no idea you were supposed to *dress up* to funerals," I told her, taking a long gulp of white wine.

She laughed and said she didn't mind, that she liked how I'd done it my way—the Vietnamese way.

I didn't know that my culture had fashioned the shape of my mourning; I didn't know that my grief could be improper.

27

November 1985—London

"What do you think of this one?" Anh asked Bianh. She held in front of her a gray blouse in silklike material with a pussycat bow.

"The color is too sad," said Bianh. "I like the blue shirt better. It looks a little more professional."

Anh listened to her friend with no objections as she was the more fashionable of the two and put the gray blouse back on its rack. They made their way to the C&A tills, where Anh handed the blue, button-down shirt and a black pencil skirt to the saleswoman. "I haven't bought clothing for myself in over two years," Anh told Bianh quietly so only she would hear. "Mostly I just wear Minh's old clothes." She and Bianh were the same shoe size, and it was agreed that Bianh would lend her a pair of small, beige heels: the outfit was already a lavish enough expense.

They made their way down Lewisham High Street all the way back to Catford. The shops had begun to decorate for Christmas, and twinkly lights, Christmas trees, and displays of snowmen and Santa Clauses gave their walk a festive spirit. "It's so crowded," said Bianh. "Everyone's doing their Christmas shopping already."

As they walked and talked, Anh's nervous mind eased, and she momentarily forgot about the interview awaiting her on Monday. After her fight with Minh last winter, she had gradually started to consider her options and decide what she could do beyond sewing blouses in a damp and cold warehouse. The truth was, it wasn't entirely by her own volition that she was looking for a new career path. Slowly but surely, the need for seamstresses was waning in London. More and more companies were outsourcing their businesses abroad, to India and China and even Vietnam. "Isn't that ironic?" she told Bianh as they passed the Sainsbury's. "Maybe if we'd stayed in Vietnam, they'd be hiring me right now." Her colleagues were diminishing at a rapid pace, the warehouse becoming quieter each day. The least efficient ones were the first to be let go, and before it became her turn, Anh decided to act.

Since the summer, she had spent almost all her free time taking part in an employment training program that the Refugee Council had provided. Once a month, she would make the journey to their offices in Stratford, which always reminded her of going into the administration offices at Kai Tak and Sopley, leaving with either devastating or wonderful news. She would have career sessions with her advisor,

Julian, a kind man with a bald head and a lengthy, untamed beard.

"I'm good at taking directions. And I'm good at keeping organized," she'd told him at their first meeting. "I used to be good at math at school, but I haven't practiced in a while," she added hesitantly, embarrassed.

"That's good," he'd told her. "It's much easier to teach someone math than to teach someone how to take directions and be organized." He leaned back in his chair, smiling. He was the one who had secured the job interview for her, for a secretary position at an accounting firm near St. Paul's Cathedral. He was about the age of her father at the time she had last seen him, and she wondered if she would have had those same conversations with her father if he was still alive, what kind of father he would have been to the adult she had become. "We can give you the skills you're missing to make you highly employable," Julian said with a smile.

Each evening, she joined Thanh at their dining table as he studied harder and harder for his A-Levels, the dark rings under their eyes increasing, their focus unwavering, Minh either out or sleeping. Her homework consisted of math and English exercises that would prove useful in the working world. Instead of learning words for discussing the weather, she learned words like "assets" and "gross profit" and "income statement," a whole vocabulary that made her feel incredibly serious, a businesswoman in the making. Sometimes, Thanh would help her. "How do you say 'tỷ lệ bách phân' again?" she would ask, timid and whispering. "*Percentage*," he would answer, not looking up from his textbook.

On weekends twice a month, she had classes at the Refugee Council, where she learned bookkeeping and how to use a fax machine and answer the phone properly, trying to sound more English, more proper. She knew that her brothers didn't mind that she was away from the apartment so often. At first, she had worried that they would not be able to take care of themselves or that they would think she was abandoning them, the same as when she had left them at Ba's for the first time. "You have the council's number if you need to reach me, right?" she asked them over and over again. "Don't do anything stupid, please." But in time, she realized that they were now old enough to look after themselves and that they welcomed the breathing space— and that she welcomed it, too. She would come back, and the table would be set and dinner ready, often just leftovers, but still, there was something luxurious about coming home to a plate of food, heated by someone else. "How was your class?" Minh would ask her. It didn't escape her that he was relieved she was now focusing on her own career rather than his, that his kind questions were a way to redirect the attention. They had not mended the injuries from their fight earlier that year, the gap between them now a constant, their cordialities an act they put on so as to avoid further fights, further scars.

"Good," she would say and then tell them about what she'd learned that day.

Twice a week in the evening, she had classes, too, at the Harris Academy in Streatham. There, she would sit at a small, wooden desk, which made her feel like she was back in school. But instead of notebooks and pencils, a typewriter stood proudly on the desk, and she would spend the next hour practicing her typing along with twenty other women, the sound ringing in her ears for the whole evening. As with sewing, she was worried at first by her slowness. She spent interminable seconds looking for each key, her fingers hovering above the machine, her typing out of synch with the rhythm of her classmates. They were given a text that they had to type up, sometimes an extract from a novel, sometimes an appliance manual, and she often struggled to understand their full meaning. The teacher, Mrs. Wools, would wander in between the desks with a strict expression, looking not at her students' faces but at their fingers, correcting their positions without uttering a word. By the end of the summer, Anh could keep up with her classmates, the sound of her typing merging with theirs, her fingers no longer constantly cramped. A few times she even spotted Mrs. Wools nodding approvingly at her pace, the hint of a smile hiding behind her red lipstick.

Anh went up to Bianh's apartment, which she shared with two other women from their old clothes factory in Hackney, to pick up her beige heels, practicing walking in them as Bianh laughed at her clumsy steps. "Just hold your head high!" she told her. "You'll get the hang of it in no time." They hugged goodbye, Bianh wishing her luck for the interview. "You'll be great," she said. "They'd be crazy not to hire you." Anh finished the walk back to her apartment alone, holding her coat close to her as she was shivering, because of either the cold or her nervousness, or both.

It was dark and the pubs were starting to fill, beer flowing down the streets of Catford. She walked by a street vendor who sold Christmas trees and on a whim bought one, the cheapest and smallest one he had but nonetheless a Christmas tree. She carried it all the way home, its needles prickling her skin as she stumbled up the flight of stairs. Her brothers gasped as she entered apartment 3B. "Is it real?" Thanh asked, reaching over and seizing it from her arms. The smell of pine wound its way through the apartment, and after a lengthy discussion, they settled on placing the tree by the window, to the left of the dining table. Minh and Thanh went to the nearby Salvation Army shop and came back with decorations, and they spent that evening adorning the tree with balls and stars, with twinkly lights and tinsel.

28

Dao

Anh is starting to look like Ma, she has the same straight
nose and wavy hair. Thanh and Minh are real grown-ups,
and I wonder which one I would have looked like more,
if I, too, would be taller than Dad and gotten buttons all
over my face like Thanh.

I wonder what kind of student I would have been.
     Serious and studious like Duc

   Or funny and chatty like Thanh

       Or gone like Minh.

I roam around like a bee playing my favorite game, insert-
ing myself into their lives.

       Imagining that I, too,

am now a true Londoner,

that I, too, am alive.

But sometimes I get overwhelmed when I realize
it has no ending.

That I exist only as a phantom limb

Of what our family could have been.

Ma said that I had to stop with my game, that I should
instead go play with Mai and Van. She told me that we
had to give Anh, Thanh, and Minh some space, that now
that they were adults, we had to stop taking care of them
so much.

After, she said that I was mad and morose, so I decided to
go wandering on my own.

I went swimming in the deepest corner
of the Coral Sea

among the whales and jellyfish,
the starfish and dolphins
swimming all around me.

I thought how it was the same water that had held me

and my family
        in our dying breaths.

            And after that, I wanted to leave.

So I went back to the void, to Ma and Dad, to Mai and
Van and Hoang. We embraced, and for a second, I swear
I felt their skins on mine, Ma's perfume snaking into my
nostrils, Van's hair prickling my skin.

    For a second, I could have sworn I was alive.

29

March 1987—London

The cherry blossoms were preparing for their grand entrance onto the streets and parks of London, like dancers waiting backstage for the curtains to be drawn. The birds were singing and fluttering their wings, wood pigeons and sparrows and robins and magpies. Tom had suggested the walk after Anh told him that she'd never seen Buckingham Palace. "We can meet at Green Park station and walk through the park to get to the gates," he explained the night before over the phone. "We should be able to see the changing of the guards, too."

She had met Tom in January, at the accounting firm in which she worked. It was more than a year now since she'd left the garment factory, and she missed her friends and she missed speaking Vietnamese and the boys from the Chinese restaurant on Kingsland Road. Her new office sat on the fifth floor of a tall, white building just off Cannon Street. It had blindingly white lighting and overly low ceilings, small desks cramped in a small room that smelled of cigarettes and stale coffee. Her days were carried by the constant thrum of typing and faxes, printing sheets of paper, and phones ringing. But at least it was a proper job, with a pension and fixed hours and better pay, a job where she was the only Asian on the floor besides the Indian accountant, who sat at the other end of the room.

When Tom arrived as an auditor, his dark suit and suitcase matching his hair and his eyes, his lanky frame awkward in the cramped and busy room, everyone had turned to him and then to her. Her colleagues' eyes moved back and forth between them, seeming to say, "Another!" though she could tell he wasn't Vietnamese, his skin much paler than hers. Her boss led Tom into his office, and after ten minutes he stepped back out to ask Anh to join them. He introduced them to each other and said with a wink, "Anh will show you around the office. Maybe you can go for lunch." The two of them sat across from him, staring at their knees, their eyes not meeting.

For the next few days, Anh showed Tom around St. Paul's, taking him to lunch at the cafeteria and the sandwich shop down the street. She learned that he was from Hong Kong but was born in London. His parents had given him an English name to reaffirm his Englishness, his belonging validated each time he introduced himself. His father was a doctor at Guy's Hospital, and his parents had hoped Tom would follow in his footsteps, but he had no interest in science. "I don't like the sight of blood," he told her, wincing. "It makes me squirm." Tom was good at math though, and he had heard that auditing was well paid and offered stability in a non-stable economy, and so without thinking much more about it, he embarked on this career.

Everyone in the office had suddenly become a match-maker, finding ways for them to work together, asking Anh to show Tom how to use the printer or to explain where the nearest post office was. She knew they meant well, but she was exhausted by their meddling, drained by her colleagues' reasoning that because they were both Asian they must belong together, by their evident lack of imagi-nation. In fact, Anh was certain she and Tom would have started dating much sooner had it not been for their relent-less interference. Instead, it was only on his last day at the firm, once he had finished auditing them, that Tom asked Anh which she thought was the best Vietnamese restau-rant in London. And when she answered, "Cây Xoài, in Peckham," he replied, "We should go there together, next Saturday."

That day, she returned to apartment 3B beaming. Immediately her brothers spotted something strange in her, a lightness they were not usually privy to. "What are you smiling about?" Minh asked her. He was twenty-two now, working full-time at the Tesco down the street. He had drifted a little from his friends over the years, but he still often came home late, smelling of god-knows-what and from god-knows-where, and Anh had given up on learning about this part of his life he kept secret.

Thanh had recently started seeing a girl, Thy, who it turned out had grown up not far from Vung Tham. They had met at one of the An Viet Foundation's social events, and immediately they had bonded over memories of their villages, about how they missed the heat and even the torrential rains, how they missed looking up at the rice fields and the twinkling sky with all the stars and planets visible, not misted by pollution. "It's like our *souls* are just connected," he had told Anh that evening, and she couldn't help but let out a snort at such a clichéd phrase, at seeing her brother falling in love, much to his irritation.

Now, it was payback time for him. "Yes, Anh," he said, snickering, sensing a man was involved. "What are *you* so happy about?"

Two months later, there they were, Anh and Tom, strolling around central London, the queen just yards away. Anh was telling him about the latest changes in the office, her boss's ridiculous ties, and her new deskmate's hot lunches, which she ate while working and whose smell lingered throughout the afternoon. Anh had not dated a lot in the past few years, focusing instead on her siblings and her career, but she'd socialized enough to know that they had reached the pinnacle where small talk would no longer suffice, when she would need to begin to open up more. She always struggled at this point because it meant revealing some of the shadows that lurked unseen inside of her. She had told Tom about her family, about Kai Tak and Sopley, but only in passing, as if they were long-ago events that she didn't think about often. She could tell that he needed more from her, that he wanted to reach inside and discover the truth, find the missing pieces of the puzzle, pieces that she had disclosed to him bit by bit over the last two months.

"How come you've been in London for seven years and you've never been to see Buckingham Palace?" he asked, interrupting her office anecdotes. She didn't know how to answer, how to explain that his London wasn't the same as hers, that she was a guest here, grudgingly accepted by the government and its citizens. She didn't belong in Green Park or Buckingham Palace. She thought she needed to be accompanied by someone like him, her living visa, a stamp in her passport that justified her presence. Instead, she said, "Time flew by. We've been meaning to go but just never found the right moment." They took a few steps in silence, and she sensed his gaze on her, knew that he wasn't satisfied with her answer.

"When we were in Hong Kong, our English teacher told us that once we made it to England, we should go visit Buckingham Palace. But I guess, sometimes, it still doesn't feel like we've really made it here." Anh was being vague on purpose, unsure of her own thoughts, what she wanted to share and what she wanted to hide. Her English was fluent now, but she still felt there was a gap between her mind and her words, a broken bridge of translation.

"What do you mean?" His tone wasn't sharp but inquisitive, one of genuine curiosity.

She took her time to answer, fiddling with her thumbs, biting her lips. She thought about Minh, the oldest son of her family, and all the hopes she and her parents had placed on his shoulders, vanished. She thought about Thanh, who'd gotten his A-Levels but hadn't applied to university because he didn't have the grades to receive financial aid. Instead, he had gotten a job in the mailroom of an insurance company near her office. On his first day, they had taken the tube together, staying quiet as he held on to the metal rail, his first taste of rush hour. "At least I can start making money right away," he'd told her the night before at dinner, moving his broccoli around his plate. "Maybe it's for the best. It was stupid to think I could work in astronomy, anyway." He was disappointed and defeated, and it pained her to see his innocence and naivete fade away, as he learned to live a life of pragmatism and compromise.

"I just don't feel like we've achieved what we wanted to here, or what our parents wanted for us," she said. "I feel like . . . we can't really do any of these things, these touristy things, until we've made it."

She thought again about what the three of them had become, living in the same one-bedroom apartment, Minh sleeping on the sofa, his feet sticking out of it. Their dinners, previously filled with Thanh chatting about school and his friends, were now spent mostly in silence, Thanh and Anh tired from their day's work, Minh either high or absent. Their monthly trips to Chinatown had become scarcer and scarcer, more a chore than a joyful outing. They were sometimes acting closer to roommates than family, three adults living together out of necessity rather than want. She avoided Tom's gaze, watching the footpath as they strolled through the park, the pollen beginning to make her nose and eyes itchy.

"It's like these things should be our rewards, more than just normal activities we can do," she continued. "That side of London shouldn't be unlocked for us yet. Not until we've *truly* made it. Not until we've left our council house and have decent jobs and all that."

She sensed him testing the ground, choosing his words carefully like a matador facing a bull, assessing, like she was, what to avoid and what to say. She wasn't used to men inquiring further. Usually, they backed off right about then, as they intuited her reluctance and the distance she was carving between them. They waved a white flag and went their separate ways. But this time, she found herself hoping that Tom would fight on, that he would not surrender.

"I'm sure your parents just wanted you all to be happy, and to be together, right? Look at you—you work at a big company; you make a decent living. You've had more success than many people who are from here and who started out with a lot more."

"I guess so," she said. A boy passed in front of her, running into the arms of his mother, who lifted him high up in the sky joyfully. She continued, "But *they* didn't make it.

And sometimes I just . . . don't feel like it's right for me, or for Thanh or Minh, to wander around London doing all these fun things that they didn't get to do."

"Of course you can. You've suffered more than enough for a lifetime. You can do whatever you want here. You have the same rights as everyone else," he said. They continued walking. The birds were still singing in the trees, the bees flying around collecting nectar from the flowers that bordered the footpaths, their buzz barely audible, mingling with the sound of children playing in the nearby grass.

"But they're dead. Almost all my family is dead." She was agitated, the truth of that fact—unspoken before—stirring and stumbling out. "It doesn't feel right to enjoy myself while they're buried in some unknown plot in Hong Kong."

Tom frowned. She worried that she had said too much, that the reality of this was too much and she had scared him away. After a few seconds, he stopped walking, and she thought, *This is it. He's going to say he has to leave.* But he did not balk, just said, "You know it's not your fault though, right?"

Anh brushed her hair away from her eyes. She felt, at that moment, that he saw through her, that he understood her fears and the grief and the guilt, that he saw Mai and Van, Dao and Hoang lodged in every corner of her mind, forming an ever-present loss that both shrouded and guided her

She grasped his hand and continued walking, not saying anything, not looking at him, only moving forward.

PART III

30

October 23, 2019—Grays, Essex

It's a little before one in the morning, and Maurice Robinson is driving his truck at a reasonable speed, conscious of his tiredness. As he climbed into the driver's seat, about half an hour ago, a pungent smell reached his nostrils, but he didn't think too much of it. Already it's been a long day: he's had a six-hour drive from Holyhead to Purfleet to pick up the truck, leaving his girlfriend asleep back home in Wales, pregnant with their twins. His phone pings and he glances at it: a Snapchat message from Ronan, his boss.

RHUGUES301: Give them air quickly don't let them out

Maurice answers with a thumbs-up emoji. He drives on for a few more minutes until he finds an industrial area, a quiet, empty spot. After parking, he walks to the back of the trailer. He opens its door and is greeted by the sight of lifeless bodies on the floor, lying in their underwear, jumbled and stacked on top of one another. The heat escapes the enclosed space, the smell of death and feces, of misery and doom.

He closes the door, staggers away, and returns to the cab. He drives in a loop and calls Ronan, who tells him again to give the refugees some air. *I can't, they're all fucking dead.* Twenty-three minutes after finding the bodies, he's back at the industrial park and calls 999. *There's immigrants in the back. They're all lying on the ground. The trailer's jammed. There's approximately twenty-five. They're not breathing.*

The police and paramedics arrive. Many are young and have never seen such a distressing scene before, piles of nearly naked bodies, the stench of sweat emanating from them, and they will require therapy later. At first, the police report that the victims are Chinese nationals—of course anyone Asian-looking must be Chinese—prompting the Chinese embassy in London to release a statement: "We read with heavy heart the reports about the death of thirty-nine people in Essex, England. We are in close contact with the British police to seek clarification and confirmation of the relevant reports." On November 2, the police clarify that all the victims are in fact Vietnamese citizens.

Autopsies are carried out. Death by suffocation and hyperthermia. CCTV across Europe shows the truck traveling through France and reaching the Belgian port of Zeebrugge in the midafternoon, boarding a ferry to Essex, and being picked up by Maurice at Purfleet. A sensor details the rising temperature inside the truck's container, reaching 104 degrees Fahrenheit during the sea crossing. Footage from a camera at the industrial park shows a cloud of steam erupting from the trailer the moment Maurice opens the door. By the time they'd reached the promised land—England—the passengers were already dead.

Inside the trailer, as the migrants died an excruciating death, some had tried to pierce open the roof with a metal pole but lacked the strength. Most had stripped to their underwear. Tran Hai Loc and Nguyen Thi Van, a married couple who had left their two children in Vietnam, held hands on the floor, and are found by the paramedics a few hours later in that same position. Some tried to send texts and voice notes to their families, but without reception inside the trailer, these remain unsent.

Maybe going to die in the container, can't breathe any more dear, typed Pham Thi Ngoc Oanh. At 7:37 p.m., Nguyen Tho Tuan recorded the following message to his parents: *It's Tuan. I am sorry. I cannot take care of you. I am sorry. I am sorry. I can't breathe. I want to come back to my family. Have a good life.* In the background, men and women can be heard coughing and gasping for air; someone says, *Come on, everyone. Open up, open up.*

Just over a year before, eighteen-year-old Hoang Van Tiep asked his parents if he could travel to the UK with his cousin Nguyen Van Hung. They'd safely made it to

France but heard of lucrative job opportunities in the UK, on cannabis farms or in nail salons or restaurants. They would purchase the VIP package to get there, he assured his parents, traveling in a private car, not in a truck container. All he needed was £10,500 to pay the smugglers, which his parents would have to borrow or mortgage their house for. Finally, Van Tiep's parents relented.

His father, Hoang Van Lan, later tells the BBC, "I don't know what happened, but something must have changed in their plan, or he was scammed." Pham Thi Lan, his wife, agrees. "No one would choose to travel in such a dangerous way."

Initially, Maurice Robinson tells the police he didn't know he was carrying people in the truck. "He is one hundred percent innocent," a close friend explains to a broadcaster. "I'm telling you now, he wouldn't have known those people were in the back." Shortly after, Maurice confesses his knowledge, having been promised £60,000 for the smuggling run. He is sentenced to thirteen years and four months in prison. His boss, Ronan Hughes, is sentenced to twenty years, on thirty-nine counts of manslaughter and conspiring to bring people into the country unlawfully.

In the months after the incident, the demand for smugglers continues, and in return, they increase their prices. They need to be paid more, they argue, to guarantee safe passage.

31

Her youngest daughter, Jane, had come back from Leeds for Ba's funeral. Ba had passed away peacefully in her sleep at Duc's house, just shy of her hundredth birthday, her mind still sharp, still filled with memories of Vietnam. She was the closest family member that Anh had lost since her parents and siblings, close not by blood but by affection and experience. This time her grief was of a different kind, one that was deeply sorrowful but also celebratory of a life lived in full. It lacked the violence and brutality of the loss she had experienced over her family's passing. This was not a life cut short; this was not a cruel death.

Anh had hoped that after the ceremony, she and Jane would spend some quality time together. But instead, her twenty-two-year-old daughter spent her days holed up in her room, reading hefty books with extravagant words in their titles, "metaphysics" and "aesthetics" and "applied ethics."

Philosophy, she had wanted to study. What a useless degree to have. What kind of job do you get with that? Philosopher? "This isn't ancient Greece," Anh had told her.

Lily and Will were here, too, her two older children, twenty-three and twenty-five, all with English names that their teachers could easily pronounce but that could also be uttered in Vietnamese, without *r*'s blocking the way. She had spent twenty years caring for them, feeding and cleaning them, comforting and reprimanding them. She had given up her career after Lily's birth, becoming a full-time mother.

She still worried that she hadn't done enough for her brothers, and particularly Minh. She had been married for twenty-seven years now, further drifting from Minh after she moved out of the Catford apartment. His temperament became moodier in the years that followed, perhaps because he resented her going away, even though it meant he could sleep on their bed instead of the sofa now that he was the eldest in the household, Thanh inheriting the living room couch. She couldn't quite leave them to stand on their own two feet without her conscience nagging her, but she conceded that it was time, that their apartment was not made for three adults. And she also thought, if only timidly, that she deserved some happiness. She had worked hard in every aspect of her life since she was a child; she had become an adult overnight, experiencing more pain than most people would in a lifetime. Yes: she deserved a slightly bigger home, with the man she loved.

To assuage her guilt, and because she missed them, she called her siblings every week and invited them to her new house, only a little farther north in the city. "We have a spare room for you," she would say on the phone. "You can sleep over." While Thanh came, telling her anecdotes of his day at work or asking for relationship advice, Minh often had excuses, a late shift or a party or "too tired." Over the years the wedge between them grew, as she let him slip away and her family expanded, shifting her focus. In what seemed like the blink of an eye, she had three young children, all with different eating habits and sleeping times, juggling nursery pickups and dinner and sometimes volunteering at the An Viet Foundation. Soon she saw Minh only two or three times a year for the Tết and their family's' giỗ. He hadn't married and he was still in Catford, empty bottles badly hidden behind his garbage can the few times she had been to visit. "I had friends over last night," he would say, following her glance. But she never heard more about these enigmatic friends and suspected they might be made-up. He managed the Tesco down the street now, but beside that, his life, how he spent his evenings or weekends, was a mystery to her.

Thanh had made a life for himself, with his wife, Thy, and their two children, now ten and thirteen, in a council house in Lewisham. A life with a tedious office job at the same insurance company where he had started his professional career, but a job that paid the bills. He had long given up on his astronomy ambitions, though he had plastered his children's bedroom with wallpaper illustrating outer space, planets and spaceships, comets and stars filling their walls and dreams both in sleep and, Thanh hoped, in life.

Anh had wanted more for them, and she worried that if only she had been stricter or more encouraging, they could have achieved more, always more. Minh could have blossomed into a businessman, an entrepreneur, anything really, if she hadn't been so scared to hear him say, "You're not Ma." He could have made more money, have had a job that he enjoyed if only she'd helped him with his homework or spent more money on his education. In remorse, she gave time over to her children, and sometimes, she looked back and thought that her whole life, really, had been devoted to her family. First to her brothers, and now to her children. She had spent forty years looking after others, putting her needs in second place, and she knew that it had been worth it.

Lily was a financial analyst in Canary Wharf, living in an apartment walking distance from the family nest. She would drop by regularly, for dinner and movie nights, always bringing home-baked goods with her, banana bread or brownies. Will worked in a big marketing firm and was dating a lovely girl from Devon, a lawyer, and they came for lunch every Sunday, Anh preparing phở or roast beef. On those afternoons, Anh sat at the head of the table and listened to her son explaining his latest campaign or heard about Lily's impending promotion. And she thought that yes, it had all been worth it in the end. She and Tom had raised a family that was secure, both financially and in their love for one another.

But philosophy, that wasn't what she had in mind for Jane, that was not part of the plan. She had worried about drugs and alcohol, about bullies and racists, but she hadn't thought to worry about Plato and Aristotle, Kant and Marx sweeping her daughter away. Anh imagined Jane hanging out with stoner friends, debating the meaning of life and life beyond death, and she thought, What an incredible waste of time. For her, life was what it was; the afterlife, whatever you wanted it to be. She didn't object too much, though. She didn't want to be a cliché— the immigrant parent, the tiger mom. And so, with her husband's encouragement, Anh gave Jane her blessing to study at Leeds, mentally preparing for her life of unemployment.

Her children knew where Anh came from, and they knew about the war, but she hadn't told them her whole story. She hadn't told them about the dockyard and the morgue, about the fishermen climbing onto their boat. "What's the point," she thought. "It'll only distress them." "What's that?" friends or old colleagues would sometimes ask her when she explained to them that she was one of the Vietnamese boat people. She would give a brief recap: Vung Tham, then Hong Kong, then Sopley, then London, her parents and siblings not making it. "You should write your memoir," they would then conclude. But living through those events had been enough; she had no desire to relive them through retelling, not after the years she'd spent shoving them to the back of her mind. Sometimes, when she saw the eyes of the person widen as she told them her story, the sudden urge to make it known would arise deep within her. British people were always surprised to learn that the country they lived in contained people with this story, contained this history. She wondered if it was her responsibility to pass it on, that if she didn't, it would fade completely, a page of the past erased.

However, the urge would die out quickly, and instead she kept these memories locked away, but they would jump out at the most unexpected moments. A random act or smell would bring back a deeply hidden memory that she didn't know she still held. The first day she dropped Will off at the nursery, she hugged him goodbye and turned around to leave. After a few steps back, she turned around again to wave, and instead of Will she saw Dao waving back at her, the same wave he had given her when she had left Vung Tham. She called her work to say she was sick and spent the day collapsed in bed, shaken to her core by this vision of the last time she had seen her baby brother. The next day, she asked Tom if he could take care of nursery drop-offs, regretful of the distance she was etching between her and the children, of removing this normally tender moment from their lives and hers.

Tom was still working, having moved up the ladder of his company from accountant to finance director. So during the day she was mostly alone, but she didn't feel lonely or bored. Bianh lived not too far away, and they still went over to each other's houses, just like they had almost forty years ago, their children nearly the same age. "We've come pretty far, haven't we?" Bianh, who still ran her small clothing business, told her one day as they were having tea in Anh's garden. "We didn't do so bad in the end." Anh took a sip from her cup, looking out at her hyacinths and roses, all in perfect shape, and said, "I guess we didn't."

She liked taking care of their garden. Over the years she had planted hollyhocks and rambling roses, cosmos and geraniums, and her favorite, peonies. She took advantage of Lily and Will being there to help with the weeding. "We need to prepare the beds for spring," she told them, handing them gloves. "Where is your little sister?"

"She's still in her room," Will said, pulling at a tenacious root. "She said she's busy working."

Anh rolled her eyes and went upstairs. "Jane!" she shouted. "Come help us with the garden, please. We've barely seen you today."

Jane emerged from her room, zombie-like, still in her pajamas, looking somewhat aghast. "Sorry, Mum," she said. "I was just finishing up something. I'll come down."

"You need to put on some clothes," Anh said. "It's almost noon!"

Her daughter seemed reluctant about something, still holding her bedroom doorknob, her feet wandering in and out of the door frame.

"Sorry," Jane said, hesitantly, looking up at her mother. "I was just reading about this . . . island."

"You want to go on holidays? Again?" Anh asked. "With what money? Aren't you already going on that trip to Spain with your friends?"

"No, no, Mum, I was just in an internet rabbit hole," Jane said, going back in her room, shutting her door. "I'm coming down. Need to change first."

She came down ten minutes later. "Look who's finally decided to join," Will said. "We're already halfway done." He handed her a small shovel.

They set to work together, Lily calling her mum every time a worm made its way out of the earth. "I'm sorry!" she would say, grimacing, as Anh finished shoveling the earth for her, rolling her eyes. "They're just so disgusting."

"Back in Vung Tham, my sisters and I would play with them and feed them to the chickens," Anh said. "You kids are way too precious."

Jane was focused, not on the earth that she was leisurely tossing but rather on her thoughts, her lips moving as if thinking out loud. Anh made her way toward her.

"You're making a mess!" Anh said. "Look at your T-shirt."

Jane stared down at her white shirt splattered with earth and brushed it down.

"Sorry, sorry. I'm not very good at this, am I?" she asked.

"No," Anh said, removing the last bits of soil from her daughter's clothes. "You've always been more of the indoor type." She turned her attention to the forsythia bush next to her daughter and started pruning.

Jane came and stood next to her, rubbing the forsythia petals with her fingers distractedly. "Mum," she said. "Have you ever thought of reconnecting with people from your village?" She wiped her forehead with her sleeve. "Aren't you curious to see what they're up to?"

Anh looked at her inquisitive daughter. Of course, the thought had crossed her mind. Bianh and Duc were both on Facebook, and they had managed to find a few childhood friends on there, urging her and her siblings to do the same. But Anh had never crossed that threshold, partly because she was bad with computers, and partly out of fear of what she might find. She was happy now. What was the point of opening a door to her past? She knew that Thanh and Minh were here and that her parents, Mai, Van, Dao, and Hoang were dead. That was enough for her.

Before Anh had time to gather herself, Jane said, "I'll set you up with an account. You don't have to use it if you don't want to. But it's really easy, you'll see."

Will came to over to them, his hand resting on his large shovel.

"What's for lunch?" he asked.

And Anh told him that if he had helped with the cooking, he would know.

*

In the paper "Family Approach with Grandchildren of Holocaust Survivors" (*American Journal of Psychotherapy* 57, no. 4, 2003), the authors give several clinical observations about the families of Holocaust survivors, made during therapy sessions. They conclude that the children of Holocaust survivors are more vulnerable to psychological distress and to post-traumatic stress disorder, as compared to the general population.

Children of Holocaust survivors learned to neglect their own feelings, to regard their own problems and anxieties as unimportant compared to those of their parents. They rapidly realized that their most important task was to be a "good son" or "good daughter." However, they soon became aware that no matter how hard they tried to achieve this goal, they would never

**fully satisfy their traumatized caregivers. They were
vulnerable, therefore, to feelings of helplessness.**

Transgenerational trauma, the idea that trauma can be
transferred through generations, has been documented
in an array of people—the descendants of those enslaved,
survivors of war, victims of abuse, and refugees. The
event in and of itself can't be passed down, of course.
Rather it is the lingering symptoms that descendants
inherit. The mother's anxiety or drug abuse, the father's
violent outbursts or depression. Behaviors that children
witness and adopt or are disturbed by, creating a vicious
circle of distress.

The first time I saw my therapist, she asked me about
my family background, so I told her about my mother.
I told her about my grandparents and the four baby siblings fished out of the sea. I told her about the war, about
the pirates and the camps. How those events loomed in
my head but were rarely discussed, how I had only heard
snatches of them over the years, from my mother and my
father, my uncles and my cousins. I told her that sometimes Mum would get quiet and distant, going from loving
to aloof in an instant, as if afraid to mother us.

Once I had finished talking, and she had scribbled her
notes, she looked up from her notebook, her glasses too
low on her nose, her expression kind. "Your family heritage

is one of death," she said. She told me that I was weighted down by this heritage I had been reluctantly given, that because I did not know it in full, it had fallen on me to complete, my imagination running havoc. I was drowning in a sea of scars and ill-mended wounds, of ghostly visions of the war and the deceased.

After our session, I went for a walk across the Rye, digesting what I'd been told. I was surprised by the relief I felt, that I was not angry or troubled but rather determined. My therapist had closed the session by suggesting I see a GP for a prescription, and so when I got home, I scheduled an appointment.

"I'm going to prescribe you an antidepressant for chronic depression and anxiety," the GP said, once I was in her consultation room, "twenty milligrams of escitalopram for now, one pill a day. We'll check in in a month and increase dosage if the side effects are manageable."

As the pharmacist handed me the medication, I felt that I had begun to rise up to the surface.

32

February 2016—Peckham

It was just Anh and Jane in the home, and they were both quiet. With Lily and Will, conversations rolled freely, their relationship with Anh easy. But with Jane, things were different. They had diverging worldviews, Jane romantic and sensitive, Anh pragmatic and thick-skinned but both, perhaps, stubborn in their ways. When Jane was six years old, she used to wake Anh up in the middle of the night and say, "Mum, I'm scared of dying," before wedging herself in between Tom and Ahn in the bed. At the time, Anh had been impatient; she didn't want to hear about death at night, not after the sleepless ones she'd already spent doing so. Anh would remember Mai slipping into her bed back in Vung Tham because she was scared, a fear that was warranted and real during the war, not like Jane's anxieties that arose from an overbearing imagination. Half asleep, she would turn her back on Jane and say, "You're being childish. Go back to bed."

Looking back, she regretted her moments of impatience. She had tried hard to be strong for her family, to conceal her own sorrows and worries as much as possible. She had raised her children with a childhood so very different from hers, one that was better in every way. But there was something about their early lives that she couldn't relate to; their existence was so blissful, so peaceful that it subconsciously made her fear something bad was bound to happen. Or perhaps her children were simply spoiled, their tantrums over not getting the latest Barbie or Pokémon cards preposterous when Thanh's pain had been about not having any photographs of his dead parents and siblings. "Not today," Anh would say, snatching the toys from her children's hands in the shop. "We're not made of money."

Even though she had tried to protect her children from distress by withholding the most gruesome parts of her experiences, she realized some things must have filtered through, through her behavior, through the pores of her skin, perhaps, or through some untold bond between mothers and their children.

Jane sat eating breakfast while on her laptop. Over her shoulder, Anh saw an encyclopedia page titled "Operation Wandering Soul" on her screen. Jane stared at the page attentively and after a while shut the laptop down. "Well, that was a weird tactic," she muttered. Anh didn't inquire, not willing to hear about another philosophical theory or debate, her ears still ringing from the time Jane had tried to explain Schrödinger's cat to her.

"I'm going to go meet some friends," Jane said, finishing her coffee. "We're going to the Tate. I won't be home too late." She put her empty mug and cereal bowl in the dishwasher and went upstairs to get ready.

Anh thought about calling Bianh to go for lunch, or perhaps doing some cleaning around the house. She could call up Thanh and suggest meeting during his lunch break. It had been a while since she'd seen him, and her empty home made her nostalgic for their days cramped in Catford, on top of one another. Funny how time romanticizes the past. If someone had told her thirty years ago she would come to miss that apartment, she would think they were mad.

She was debating her options, but at the back of her mind were Jane's words. Have you ever thought of reconnecting with people from your village? Aren't you curious what they're up to? Jane had made Anh a Facebook account the week before, once they came in from the garden, and it lay dormant, her childhood perhaps only a few clicks away. Anh didn't send friend requests, didn't click "like" or write comments on family photos. She thought about Vung Tham and her childhood friends, who were now in their midfifties like her. In her mind they were still young, like figurines trapped in a snow globe, frozen in eternal youth. And she didn't want to unfreeze that time, didn't want to be burdened with their loss of innocence.

Still, she couldn't help but be curious about something, something that was not so much about opening a door to her past than one for her future. In all the years that had gone by, she had put so much of her adolescence to bed. But there was still something eating at her, that grew the more her other aches diminished, and that had grown even bigger once her children had left the family nest and she finally had time to herself to breathe. She opened her computer, took a deep breath, and typed "Nam Phan" in the search bar. But there were many Nam Phans, and she wasn't sure if she would recognize his picture, wasn't even sure he was alive anymore, let alone on Facebook. Resolved now, she decided to try Google and typed in "Nam Phan New Haven" and then "Nam Phan New Haven Son Lam," which was the village where she had been told her uncle had lived, not far from Vung Tham.

She wasn't certain what she wanted, exactly. On top of sheer curiosity, there was a desire for forgiveness, to be able to look at her uncle, even if just his photograph, and say, "It wasn't your fault." Or perhaps it was a way to forgive herself, perhaps she wanted to see into his life in New Haven and reassure herself that by saying, "It's just us," back in the immigration office in Kai Tak, she hadn't doomed her brothers but rather blessed them with the best possible life open to them. She had thought about what would have happened if they had gone to America. They wouldn't have met Duc or Ba. She wouldn't have met Tom. She wouldn't have had Will or Lily or Jane. She knew that Minh held bitterness, that he believed he would have been happier in the States. "Maybe by now I would have a whole restaurant empire!" he had told her and Thanh last year at Tết, half joking, half serious. "The grass is always greener," Thanh had answered, shrugging. "Who knows, maybe we would have all been worse off."

Anh thought that there was reassurance in this unknown. That there were an infinite number of ways their lives could have turned out, and they owed their lives to good currents and a Buddha statue, kind strangers and luck: lots of luck. Each instance, each decision and action had brought them here, to London—and she was glad they had.

The search results appeared, and as she scanned down the list, she struck upon the unexpected: a forum for Vietnamese boat people, for people on the lookout for long-lost family members. The website was rudimentary and outdated, a simple blog interface, but it held page after page of people like her, people from all over Vietnam, North to South, dotted across the world, Australia and Germany and Canada, looking for their aunts or nephews or cousins. She leaned back on her chair, dazzled, taking it all in. She was overwhelmed by a feeling of connectedness, realizing she wasn't alone in her desire. She read page after page of threads, down and down, finally looking up Vung Tham and Son Lam until she saw that a man called Thach Phan had posted in 2014 a long note that began:

My father, Nam Phan, my mother, Thi Ngoc Phan, my brother, and I left Son Lam in 1975, a few months before the fall of Saigon. We spent two months in Kai Tak refugee camp in Hong Kong and got resettled to New Haven, USA . . .

Anh scrolled down through the post, which detailed their life in America, a life where the Phans had opened one of the first nail salons in Connecticut and managed to send their sons to college to study medicine and law. Her stomach dropped. This was a life that she should have had, a life that carried her last name. She scrolled and at the very bottom, the message read:

My father had a brother, Hut Phan. He lived in Vung Tham with his wife and seven children. They were supposed to join us in New Haven in 1978, but they didn't make it. My father contacted Kai Tak the next year, and they told him that they had found their bodies and buried them. But they said that three of the children were still alive. They gave my father the contact details of the camp in Britain they had been resettled to, but my father was too ashamed to make the call. I think he blamed himself for his brother's death, and for the death of his wife and children. By the time he did call, a few years later, the camp no longer existed, and he gave up on finding them. He only told my brother and me this in 2009, before he

passed away. He couldn't remember their names, only his brother's. If anyone knew any families in Vung Tham in the 1960/70s that sound like this one, please get in touch.

Anh called up to Jane in her room, her voice quivering. But as usual, her daughter was wearing headphones and couldn't hear her. Anh shouted again, but once more her daughter didn't answer. She climbed up the stairs, determined, bursting into her daughter's room, the laptop open in her hands, held out in front of her. "Mum, you have to knock!" Jane said. And in response, Anh asked, "Can you help me write a message?"

*

Over the Christmas break, I read the *Iliad*. It was one of those books that had been on my reading list since before I'd even become a reader, along with *Ulysses* and *In Search of Lost Time* and *Infinite Jest*, one of those books that I'd picked up many times before, browsing through its many pages and thinking, "No, it's not the right time," before putting it back on its shelf unread. But this time, I picked it up and kept on reading.

The story begins in the ninth year of the Trojan war. Achilles withdraws from battle following a quarrel with Agamemnon, commander of the Achaean army. As a result, the Greek army gets slaughtered by the Trojans, suffering consequent losses, but Achilles refuses to fight, his pride hurt too deeply. When the Trojan prince Hector kills his most loyal companion—and hinted lover—Patroclus, Achilles becomes mad with sorrow. He rejoins

the battle and goes on a killing spree, clogging the Sca-
mander River with slain Trojans, angering its god. Finally,
he kills Hector, fulfilling his vengeance. "By your life, I beg
you, by your knees, your parents—don't let dogs eat me by
Achaean ships," says Hector, as his dying wish. "Send
my body home again, so Trojans and Trojans' wives can
bury me, with all the necessary funeral rites."

It struck me how it was not pride nor honor nor lust for war
that drove Achilles back to battle but rather grief. I thought
about my mother's stories of the war that she used to tell
Lily and me at bedtime. She told us about her grandfather,
who had fought with the French in Indochina. When she
was a young child, he claimed that he had spent the war
dodging gunshots instead of producing them. The one time
he opened fire with the desire to kill was after he had seen
his closest comrade fall on the battlefield, like a sparrow
diving headfirst back to earth, a bullet through his lungs.
My great-grandfather held him as he lay dying, his mouth
filling with blood. "He killed ten soldiers that day," Mum
said. "I don't know if it's true, though. He was a storyteller."
    Once the firing had stopped, my great-grandfather
dragged the body back to camp and buried his friend in a
nearby field.

After killing Hector, Achilles continues to mourn, weeping alongside the Achaeans, refusing to wash until he has

buried Patroclus. The night following the funeral feast, he is woken up by the ghost of his friend, begging him to hold his funeral soon so that his soul can enter the Land of the Dead. "Bury me, quickly—let me pass the Gates of Hades," the ghost says. "They hold me off at a distance, all the souls, the shades of the burnt-out, breathless dead, never to let me cross the river, mingle with them . . . They leave me to wander up and down, abandoned, lost at the House of Death with the all-embracing gates."

Achilles buries him the next day, building a pyre a hundred feet in length on which to burn his body, along with sacrificial dogs and sheep and stallions and twelve Trojan soldiers.

There's another story my mum told me: as a teenager, I suffered bad bouts of sleep paralysis. During the darkest moments of the night, my eyes would open, and I would lie on my bed, conscious but unable to move. I would see, clear as day, a dark figure enter my room, the door creaking, the man's footsteps approaching, his hands shuffling on my blanket. My whole body would be shaking but still I lay there paralyzed, convinced this was my end, convinced this was real. But as in all nightmares, I would wake up with a jolt right before his hands reached me. "It's just the dead coming to say hello," my mum told me one morning, after I'd told her about my night. "We call it *bóng đè* in Vietnam. Maybe it was your uncles or aunts, or grandparents." I looked at her, tired, incredulous. "Don't be afraid of them," she said, kissing my forehead.

Following Patroclus's funeral, Achilles's grievous wrath continues. He abuses and defames Hector's body, repeatedly dragging it around the tomb of his friend as dust rises around him, denying Hector his final wish.

Once when I was little, I took a longan from the altar during our ancestor ceremony, before the incense had finished burning. "Don't do that, Jane!" my uncle told me as I held the fruit in my hand, its skin half peeled, its juices running. "Do you want to disrespect the ancestors?" He hadn't said it with venom, more panicked than angry, but I was ashamed. I went up to my room quickly, whispered, "Sorry," and burst out crying, distraught. I hadn't meant to offend; I hadn't meant to defame.

Mum came to see me as I lay on my bed, my pillow wet with tears, and she told me yet another story. "My little sisters and I used to do the same thing, back in Vung Tham," she said, pulling me up from the bed, smoothing my hair. "We would take turns snatching lychees on our tippy toes, careful not to get caught. I'm sure they wouldn't mind."

Finally, on the twelfth day following his death and with the help of the gods, Hector's father, Priam, king of Troy, makes the perilous journey to the Achaean camp. He comes to beg Achilles for the body of his son, so that he, too, can give him a proper funeral. "Remember your own father," he says, trying to appeal to Achilles's sympathy, "who's as old as me, on the painful threshold of deadly old age." Achilles, swayed by visions of his own father, relents and decrees a twelve-day cease-fire to give the Trojans time to prepare the funeral.

It was past midnight by the time I'd finished the *Iliad*, and the whole house was asleep besides Mum and me, the night owls of the family. I came down to the kitchen, and she was drinking her tea on the dining table, doing a crossword puzzle. She looked up as she heard my footsteps. "Oh, you're still awake," she said.

I poured myself a glass of water. "I was just finishing my book," I said as I took a sip.

We stayed silent, the scribble of her pen merging with the sounds of the night. I wondered what kept her awake all these nights. I wondered if she had nightmares, too, or ghostly visitations. If she was like Priam, haunted by her family's burial, or rather its lack. "Why do you go to bed so late?" I asked, finally. She detached her eyes from her paper, looked up at me, and then looked down again.

"I don't know," she said, shrugging. "I've always been this way."

This answer opened more questions than it closed. I wanted to know more. I wanted to delve deeper and unearth the reason, all the reasons, but instead I just nodded—scared of intruding, of angering her. I rinsed and dried my glass, putting it back on its shelf.

"Goodnight, Mum," I said, leaving the room and my thoughts behind, shutting the door.

33

June 2019—Ho Chi Minh City, Vietnam

Anh watched the coffins slowly glide into the cremation chamber, her parents first, then Dao, Mai, Van, and Hoang last, his casket hardly bigger than a shoebox. Her baby brother's cremains were barely visible in the plastic bag that the technician handed over to them. She wondered which ash contained his tiny fingers, which ash contained his stubby legs and toes. She was surprised how these thoughts came to her, more pragmatic than sorrow filled, the difference in appearance too wide for her to fully fathom what she held in her hands.

She and her brothers, Tom, and their children had flown in from Heathrow the night before. As soon as she stepped off the airplane, the heat and humidity dizzied her, taking her by surprise, as if an old friend that she could no longer recognize was embracing her.

Their cousin Thach had arranged for the bodies to be

transferred from Hong Kong to Ho Chi Minh. They had kept in regular contact over the past three years since Anh had answered his message on the forum, with Jane's help. "Hello, Thach," she had typed. "I think my brothers and I are the family you are looking for." Her brothers had objected at first. "What if he's a scammer?" Minh had said. "Or what if he's crazy?" Thanh had added. But he was not a scammer and he was not crazy, he was their cousin with an American accent who loved baseball and old cars like his father. Thach, his brother, and his mother came to visit London a year after, and they all cried as they hugged one another, as they took each other's hand into their palms, checking that they were real. Their American family gawked at Will's height, at Anh's garden and their surroundings, Jane taking them to visit Big Ben and the British Museum. "It's all stolen stuff, by the way," she said as they passed the Rosetta stone.

During their visit, Thach brought up the subject of burial. "We can make it happen, you know," he'd said over dinner. "Give them a proper resting place. Our old neighbors did it, for their parents." Anh and her brothers looked at one another. This was something that they had discussed together, privately, but had always found reasons to put it off—Anh's pregnancies or a busy work period for one of them. "Do we really want to go back?" Minh would say. "We didn't exactly leave on the best of terms." Anh and Thanh wouldn't say anything, looking down at their

plates or teacups, unsure whether they agreed or not. But
Thach had given the push they needed. "You will regret it
if you don't," he said. "I can contact the Kai Tak cemetery
and get things moving." And so he did.

Now, Anh was in a hurry to get it done, to get it over with.
Not out of impatience but because this was a burden that she
had carried for more than forty years, a burden that became
unbearable the more she approached the finish line. As
she saw the coffins disappear into the furnace, holding Lily's
hand, she sensed that they were taking with them a heavy
load, and when she was handed the remains, she was light
and renewed. Tom put a hand on her shoulder and kissed
the top of her head. He gestured for the children and Thach
to walk out of the room with him, Will giving his mother
a hug as he left, leaving Anh, Minh, and Thanh alone in
the crematorium. Once they were alone they laughed, hot
tears on their cheeks, indescribable tears of neither sadness
nor joy. They left the building, plastic bags in their hands.
The cremains were whiter and lighter than snow. Rays of
sunlight blinded them, and the busy streets of Ho Chi Minh
City rang in their ears, the motorbikes and bicycles almost
brushing against them, the smell of phở and bun cha rice
and traffic fumes hitting their nostrils. "It's done," Anh said.
"They're home now."

Anh had never been to Ho Chi Minh City, and even the
name seemed alien to her. In her mind, the place was still

called Saigon. For the rest of the week, she played tourist with her family, visiting Bình Tây Market and Cao Đài temple but passing on the War Remnants Museum and the Củ Chi tunnels, preferring to explore the streets, the local markets and shops. "Mum, can I get an áo dài made?" Jane asked as they passed a tailoring shop. "Alright. Lily, you can get one, too," she said. "You can wear them to your weddings," she added, barely audibly, just enough for Jane to hear and turn to her, annoyed.

Anh found she had trouble adjusting to the heat, that the humid weather made her stomach turn and head dizzy, the jet lag not helping. The locals could detect that she and her brothers were not from here, hints of English having filtered into their Vietnamese over the years. On her second day, as she was getting bánh bèo from a street stall with her daughters, the seller asked her where she was from. "Vung Tham," Anh said. "But we live in London now, in England." The woman smiled and said, "Ah, so you abandoned your country." She didn't sound bitter or vicious but matter-of-fact, her statement not up for debate. Anh didn't know how to respond, the words shutting her brain down. She just smiled back, giving the stallholder an extra 20,000 đồng out of a sense of guilt, telling her to keep the change. When Lily asked, "What did she say?" Anh replied, "Oh, nothing, she asked where we came from and said you were very pretty."

She hadn't thought of it this way. In her head, she had been the victim, her family the wronged ones, the ones

abandoned by their country, by the whole world, in fact.
She hadn't considered that the roles could be reversed,
that others could perceive it any other way. That they
could think she had run away from her country and settled in the West, returning forty years later with her family
and her wealth, a flashy heap of đồngs in her purse, her
skin no longer used to the climate. For a moment, she was
embarrassed for having turned her back on the land that
had birthed her, ashamed that she felt like a stranger and
was being treated like one. The street vendors followed
her and Tom around, trying to sell them fresh coconuts or
nón lá hats, not differentiating between her and the other
tourists. If anything, they were even more persistent with
her, using her Vietnamese as a weapon, telling her pitiful
stories of the sons they were trying to put through college.
And like any other tourist, she relented and obliged, buying more hats and coconuts and fresh mangoes than she
could carry, the guilt she held driving her spending.

The next day she ate phở for breakfast at the hotel with
her brothers while her family and Thach slept, the sun barely
risen above the horizon. It was like they were back in Kai
Tak, eating bowls of congee in the bright cafeteria before
their lessons, Anh sitting across from them, their heads lowered, as Thanh chewed with his mouth open. He Facetimed
his children and wife as they were about to go to bed back
in London. "I miss you," he told them, smiling tenderly into
the screen. Minh had the same vacant expression that he

had developed in his teenage years, which Anh blamed on the early wake-up and jet lag.

Everything had changed and nothing had changed. They were still her burden and her pride, and she still sought to protect them. As ever, she tried to hide her worries from them, except now they were older and wiser and could tell when something was bothering her, her eyes a little more idle, her fingers fidgeting with the tablecloth. "What's wrong?" asked Thanh once he had hung up his phone.

She told them about the woman at the stall, trying to laugh it off, as if the whole interaction had been trivial. "She was just jealous," Minh said with a shrug. "Of course, we didn't abandon our country. We had no choice, Anh." His words surprised her. She had always thought he was the one most adamantly against the plan, the one who thought their father had been an idiot for putting them on the boat. Her confusion must have shown on her face because Minh continued. "Do you know why Duc and Ba were alone in the UK? It's because the government raided his house one night and took his mum and dad to a reeducation camp. He only made it out safely because he was small enough to hide in the cupboard in the kitchen. And they spared Ba because she was elderly." He snorted. "As if out of respect for her." He took a sip of his phở, slurping his noodles. "Don't you see? The government was closing in on any family they suspected of being anti-Communist. And Vung Tham was near the

South, and they knew we had family in the United States because of all those letters Nam sent us and because Dad taught English. We must have been high on their list."

She knew this, of course. She remembered the hushed discussions, the neighbors disappearing, her parents' distant and nervous behavior. It wasn't her father's paranoia that had put the plan in motion; it was the reality of their situation. It wasn't desertion; it was a desperate attempt to live. "We didn't abandon anything," Thanh said. "We only did what we had to do to survive." After all these years, it was her brothers' turn to shield her. She would always feel that a trace of dishonor marked her, but she was mostly proud that they had survived, that they had managed to conjure lives for themselves from thin air. Yes, they weren't doctors or engineers or millionaires, and there would always be a part of her that wished they had achieved these things. But they had climbed a mountain of impossible odds and impending doom, and looking back, she realized that it had been a vertiginous ascent indeed.

The siblings hadn't settled on what to do with the ashes. They'd thought about releasing them in the open, about going back to Vung Tham and setting them free there. But neither Anh nor her brothers felt any desire to return to their village, the village that they had spent so much of their youth reminiscing about. It turned out it wasn't the village that they had longed for but rather the life they could have had there. Now all that remained for them in Vung Tham was the specter of this life, of their childhoods and the war. So they didn't go back, and they didn't release the ashes there because it wasn't their home anymore. Home was where they were together, the living family, the survivors. They placed the remains into six urns, two larger, red ones with gold adornments for their parents, and smaller wooden ones for their siblings. At the airport, they said goodbye to Thach, who was returning to New Haven, promising to keep in touch and visit at Christmas.

"Oh, I almost forgot," he said. "I have a gift for you." He opened his hand luggage and took out a thick envelope, which he handed to Anh. "I found these in my father's old office. I think he kept them hidden away, but they belong to you."

She opened the envelope, and it was filled with a dozen photos of her family, of her father and mother's wedding day, of her cousins and her siblings playing together, of family dinners and celebrations. Anh thumbed through the photos, pausing on each one, until she came to the bottom of the pile. Staring up at her was the photograph of them sitting on the couch at their last Tết, the same photograph that Thanh had destroyed in anger all these years before.

"Your dad always sent my father photographs of you when we were young," Thach said. "He was really proud of you."

She could barely say thank you, too emotional to utter words. Instead, she gave Thach another hug and held the photographs close to her chest, careful not to dampen them with her tears. On the plane, she handed them to her children. "These are your grandparents, aunts, and uncles," she told them. Will grabbed the first one, a portrait of Mai and Van holding hands. "They look like Lily and Jane," he said.

"And you look like him," said Lily, showing Will a photo of a little boy in a blue ao dai, slightly too big for him, his expression stern and shy, a sack of marbles in his left hand, the village's banyan tree behind him.

"That's Dao," Anh said. "He must have been five or six, here."

Anh, Thanh, and Minh carried the remains in their hand luggage all the way to Heathrow, where it was decided that they would take turns looking after them. Minh took them home with him first as he was the oldest male of the family. Anh couldn't help but hope that their presence would influence him, that they would curtail his drinking and whatever else he shouldn't have been doing. "You'll look after them, but don't forget that they're also looking after you, now," she told him, having faith that he would understand the meaning beneath her statement, but he just nodded absentmindedly, not taking her words in.

They said goodbye in front of the taxi station, Anh

getting into a cab with her children and Tom, Thanh and Minh taking the train together.

"We'll see you soon," said Thanh. "I'll bring the children over before they go back to school."

And so now the whole family was in London, because London was where they were, and where they were was home.

34

Dao

As I watched them digging up my grave, I panicked, until Dad explained what was happening.

They kept us in our boxes, and like this our bodies took a plane for the first time.

What an odd feeling it is, to see your body on the move without you,

Like a video with delayed sound.

But as I saw my casket, it sunk in deeper than it ever had,

That I was no longer of this Earth.

We arrived in Saigon in a huge car and a cortege. It was

our time to shine, I thought, and Mai and Van were excited like me.

Even though I cannot feel, I could tell the room was very hot.

> I saw my casket burning and my body with it
>> Smothered by flames.

And all that remained of it
> Was a small pile of white powder.

I didn't need
to wander anymore
or to play games.
It was time to rest.

I am no longer a phantom limb
I am the beloved brother Dao gone too soon,
I am a real ancestor.

We are still resting, sometimes at Minh's and sometimes at Thanh's and sometimes with Anh, but it is a rest so deep that only the smell of incense can wake us up. And when it does, I know there is a meal waiting for me, a meal of caramelized braised pork and eggs, longans and rambutans, spring rolls and sauteed shrimps with ginger and scallion, steamed sea bream and stir-fried morning glories.

Once we are full, I look around the room one last time. I
look at my siblings and my in-laws and my nephews and
nieces, and I feel pride. I kiss them all goodbye, and we go
back to our long sleep.

35

April 2022—Peckham, London

It was the first week of the year that hinted at the oncoming summer, the first week in which you could leave your coat at home.

Anh was at the big Sainsbury's on Dog Kennel Hill. She grabbed some shrimp paste and oyster sauce, some steaks and pork chops, zucchini, and peppers, getting lost among the unending aisles. At the till, she picked up some flowers, white roses and pink lilies. The cashier asked her, "Where are you from?" with genuine curiosity, which endeared her to Anh more than it annoyed her. "Oh Vietnam! That's my favorite cuisine. I love phở."

Of course she did. Everyone loved phở now. Everyone loved bánh mìs and spring rolls and viet coffees. It wasn't cool to eat phở forty years ago, Anh could tell you that. But nowadays, she saw young people and businessmen slurping their noodles everywhere, from Soho to Bank, Brixton to Notting Hill. There was Bánh Bánh in Peckham and Green

Papaya in Hackney, Viet Café in Camberwell, Cây Tre in
Soho and House of Hô in Fitzrovia, and Phat Phuc in Chel-
sea. New ones were popping up every day, some good and
some not so good. She would try them out with Bianh and
the other friends she had made at the Hackney garment factory all those years ago, the ones who had followed her life
devotionally, whose children had grown up beside her own.

And then during COVID they were the enemies again,
and people covered their mouths when they crossed the
street, shouting, "Kung Flu!" at her. She watched the news
and saw women that looked like her being beaten up for
no reason, bruised adults crying in shock at the hate and
violence that was directed toward them. She talked about it
with Jane, with whom she had grown closer in the last few
years now that her teenage angst had eased, her soul lighter.
At first, she told Jane, "It's okay. I'm wearing a mask, so
people won't be able to tell that I'm Asian." But Jane told
her, "Mum, it's not the mouth that's the problem." So for a
while, she was scared at the thought of her family leaving
the house. She wore sunglasses in winter and tried not to
speak, not to reveal her Asian-ness. But then she started to
feel that it could be detected in her whole being, in the way
she walked and held her bag, as if she had a stamp on her
forehead that said, ASIAN.

Anh pitied these people. She pitied their ignorance,
their misconceptions, which blurred their minds into
oblivion. She sensed their hate and sensed their fears,
that she was the scapegoat for their emotions, she and her

family. It wasn't personal, she kept telling herself. They just don't know any better. Still, she couldn't help resenting them, remembering the hardships she had lived through to get to where she was, that her presence in this country was valid. She didn't steal anyone's job, and she didn't get in trouble with the law; she had followed all the rules and been a model citizen, and yet when people looked at her, all they saw was otherness. She tried to focus on the good things, on their neighbors who left a loaf of freshly made bread on their doormat every few weeks, or the man at the deli who always gave her children a free ice cream during the summer, even now that they were fully grown. There was goodness in the world, she thought to herself. Yes, a lot of goodness, if you looked closely.

Tom had started prepping the barbecue, and by the time she got home the coal was burning and the fire mounting. Duc and her brothers were drinking beer in the garden. Thanh's wife was keeping an eye on their roaming children, steering them away from the flames. Anh removed the flowers from their wrapping and placed them in a tall glass vase filled with water, and Lily brought it to the dining table. "They look beautiful, Mum," she said. Will helped her unpack the groceries, and together they started prepping the food; he salted the beef and pork while she chopped the zucchini and peppers into thin slices. Lily and Jane set the table, juggling stacks of plates in their hands, then brought the food over to their father so he could start grilling.

Thanh had his guitar with him and he played a few melodies, the Beatles and Françoise Hardy and Elvis, his children singing along with him while Minh and Duc looked on, smiling and drinking. The smell of smoked meat rose from the grill and filled the garden as Tom diligently fanned the flames away from his guests. Anh brought Maggi sauce and a bowl of potato chips to the table and helped herself to some orange juice. "Mum, stop working," Lily said, drawing a chair for her. "Come sit down with us."

As she took in the scene, she thought about her parents and Mai and Van, about Dao and Hoang resting on her living room altar, longans and oranges surrounding their framed photographs and Ba's. She thought about the lady who gave them rambutans in Hainan and their neighbors in quarantine, about Isabel and Mrs. Jones, about Sophie and Mr. and Mrs. Evans. She thought about how they were all in their old age now, perhaps even dead, and that she was alive, she was alive and well, her daughters and her son building their own lives, her husband grilling steaks and pork chops for her family in their garden, its roses blooming.

And it was quite a wonderful thing, she thought, to be alive.

*

I was reading *The White Album* by Joan Didion the other day. *Slouching Towards Bethlehem* is her most well-known essay collection, but I prefer *The White Album,* which focuses on California in the late 1960s and early '70s. Each time I read it I want to jump into a swimming pool, the shade of palm trees cooling the blazing sun. The titular essay begins with the sentence "We tell ourselves stories in order to live," which has become an iconic line, its renown overshadowing its meaning. The essay in question was written just after the Sharon Tate murders at the hands of cult leader Charles Manson's followers. In it, Didion describes a Hollywood brimming with paranoia and pessimism, a Hollywood that has been made aware of its own mortality, of drugs and alcohol in abundance.

Just a few weeks ago, Mum and I watched *Once Upon a Time in Hollywood* by Quentin Tarantino. In the film, he imagines an alternate reality of Hollywood, where Manson's followers decide at the last minute to murder Sharon Tate's neighbor instead. But the neighbors fight back, and the would-be murderers end up getting killed in classic Tarantino style, mauled by a dog and incinerated with a flamethrower, while Sharon Tate and her friends live. "It's too violent," Mum said as the murderers screamed for their lives, her mug of steaming tea shielding her eyes. "Next time, pick a film where no one dies." I was more bothered by the way Bruce Lee was portrayed in the film, arrogant and foolish, an unnecessary caricature drawn by the white gaze.

The next day, we went for a walk around Hyde Park to see the Rose Garden. The pollen was stirring up Mum's allergies, her eyes red and itchy and her nose runny, but she lingered in front of the cherry trees and the fountains, her pace leisurely. "It's my favorite time of the year," she said. "It's the season of renewal." For hours we walked around the gardens and then across London, not saying much, the occasional question popping up about my PhD, "Are you sure they're still hiring philosophy professors?"; the occasional comment about my sister's new boyfriend, "I like him better than the last one"; or about Will's love life, "When is he going to propose to her?"

Afterward, we went to Viet Food in Chinatown, where we ate phở and bánh xèo. "We had these in Vietnam, remember? My ma used to make them for us sometimes," she said, lifting the shrimp pancake with her chopsticks. "Hers was better, but this is pretty good, too." I ordered a beer, and at this she grimaced, still not used to seeing me drink, beer being the beverage of her brothers, and before that of her father. We took a cab home, and by the time we got back, Dad was getting ready for bed, greeting us at the door in his pajamas. I said goodnight to them both as he boiled the water for her herbal tea, and I sat back down at my desk to write.

"We look for the sermon in the suicide, for the social or moral lesson in the murder of five," Didion goes on. "We live entirely, especially if we are writers, by the imposition of a narrative line upon disparate images."

We fill in the gaps. We find stories in every little moment and gather them up readily. We imagine that the unknown isn't the worst scenario and we try to make sense of the senseless. We look for the silver linings and the whys and what-ifs and what-should-have-beens. We try to solve the puzzle, pieces scattered through time and space and the deepest corners of our memories. And what better way is there of doing that, what better way is there of processing our past, than by rewriting it?

I get paralyzed by the idea of getting something wrong, anything, any detail, so I'll look up the most banal information—"how did they cook rice in Vietnam in the 1970s"—something Mum could answer in an instant but I don't want to pester her, and so instead I watch YouTube videos showing it.

And I am overly wary of writing clichés, so much so that I hesitated for weeks before mentioning said rice on the first page of the book. I don't want to write about phở and spring rolls and nail salons and strangers saying "Ni hao" to me, and yet I'll have to at some point, because like it or not, they are integral to my story.

I wonder what to keep and what to leave, what to amend and what to destroy. Change the name of the village. Change the camps. But keep my uncle's love of music. Yes, I'll keep his guitar and his Beatles records. But I'll change their names, change their professions. Make it fiction. But do keep the deaths. Keep the bodies buried at the camp. Yes, do keep the suffering. But don't overdo it. Add some joy. Keep my mother's story of when she saw snow for the first time. Keep the way she met my father. Yes, add some joy.

Once the project looks a little more concrete, I'll casually mention to Mum that I've started writing something inspired by her story, emphasis on *inspired*, and I'll see her break into a smile.

I'll think of all the stories she has told me—stories about the war and friendly ghosts, stories to console and appease me. I'll realize that they were stories she told herself, too, that stories are a bridge between us, and I'll understand that I have uttered a wish she has held on to since long before it came to me.

We tell ourselves stories in order to live.
We tell ourselves stories in order to heal.

Jane Mai Van Leung, London, March 2023

Acknowledgments

To Matt Turner: thank you for always believing in my novel and in me; for all of your guidance, kindness, and dedication—you're the best agent I could have asked for.

To my wonderful editors, Ruby Rose Lee at Henry Holt and Kishani Widyaratna at 4th Estate: thank you for your brilliant insights, endless patience, and unwavering support—I am so grateful to have worked with you both.

To the whole Henry Holt team, especially Retha Powers, Natalia Ruiz, Amy Einhorn, Christopher Sergio, Chris O'Connell, Carol Rutan, Clarissa Long, Laura Flavin, Arriel Vinson, Caitlin O'Shaughnessy, and Omar Chapa: thank you for your passion and for all your excellent, hard work, without which this book would not exist.

To the amazing team at Rogers, Coleridge and White, particularly Peter Straus, Sam Coates, Tristan Kendrick, Stephen Edwards, Katharina Volckmer, Aanya Dave, Natasia Patel, and Laurence Laluyaux: thank you for championing *Wandering Souls* so fervently from its early days and for finding it more readers than I could ever dream of.

To the Spread the Word team, especially Bobby Nayyar and Eva Lewin, for giving *Wandering Souls* a chance; and to my London Writers Awards group, Catherine Menon, Sukh Brar, Victoria Cano, Ashani Lewis, Shereen Akhtar, and Tommy Rowlands: thank you for providing me with crucial, much-needed feedback and help during the book's inception.

Thank you to all these writers I admire so deeply who took the time to read and support this book at such an early stage. Ocean Vuong, Kawai Strong Washburn, Yara Rodrigues Fowler, Sara Jafari, Nadia Owusu, Jenny Tinghui Zhang, and many more: thank you—I am so grateful to you.

To Michal Shavit, Željka Marošević, and all my Jonathan Cape colleagues, for their generous encouragement and wisdom.

To the friends who kept me sane, cheered me on, and offered me sage advice during the whole process: Tom, Isabella, Greg, Dredheza, Maria, Hope, Duc, Jan, Angélique, Daisy, Poppy, and many more—thank you.

To Jack: thank you for being here; thank you for being you.

Finally, my eternal thanks to my family, for their love and faith: Maman, Papa, Solange, et Florence. Je vous aime fort.

About the Author

Cecile Pin grew up in Paris and New York City. She moved to London at eighteen to study philosophy at University College London, followed by an MA at King's College London. She writes for *Bad Form Review*, was long-listed for its Young Writers' Prize, and is a 2021 London Writers Award winner. *Wandering Souls* is her first novel.